JUSTIFIED MISFORTUNE

BROTHERHOOD PROTECTORS WORLD

LORI MATTHEWS

Twisted Page Press LLC

BROTHERHOOD PROTECTORS

ORIGINAL SERIES BY ELLE JAMES

Brotherhood Protectors Series

Montana SEAL (#1)

Bride Protector SEAL (#2)

Montana D-Force (#3)

Cowboy D-Force (#4)

Montana Ranger (#5)

Montana Dog Soldier (#6)

Montana SEAL Daddy (#7)

Montana Ranger's Wedding Vow (#8)

Montana SEAL Undercover Daddy (#9)

Cape Cod SEAL Rescue (#10)

Montana SEAL Friendly Fire (#11)

Montana SEAL's Mail-Order Bride (#12)

SEAL Justice (#13)

Ranger Creed (#14)

Delta Force Rescue (#15)

Montana Rescue (Sleeper SEAL)

Hot SEAL Salty Dog (SEALs in Paradise)

Hot SEAL Hawaiian Nights (SEALs in Paradise)

Hot SEAL Bachelor Party (SEALs in Paradise)

For Beverly Pattison
A fan from the very beginning.

As always my heartfelt thanks goes out to many people. My deepest gratitude my editors, Corinne DeMaagd and Heidi Senesac for their patience and guidance; my cover artist, Lyndsey Llewellen, Llewellen Designs for making my story come alive: my virtual assistant who is a social media guru and all-round dynamo, Susan Poirier. My friends who talk me off the ledge on more occasions than I care to admit: Janna MacGregor, Suzanne Burke, Stacey Wilk and Kimberley Ash. My mother and my sisters whose support I value so highly. My husband and my children who not only support me but add to my stories in innumerable ways. Thanks for all of your great ideas! You all are my world. A special heartfelt thanks goes out to you, the reader. The fact you are reading this means my dreams have come true.

A special thanks to Elle James for trusting me with her characters and her world. I am profoundly grateful.

CHAPTER 1

SUNNY PULLED her silver BMW into the lot behind the diner. Chances were good it would be dark when she left, so she parked directly under the streetlight. It was unfortunate the streetlight was in the farthest corner of the lot next to the fence, but she certainly didn't want a repeat of yesterday.

Sunny looked all around before exiting the car and hustling to the back entrance. She flew in through the door of the diner and barreled directly into Wilson Montgomery, the short order cook.

"Hey there, Monkey. Where are you going in such a hurry?" Wilson said as he caught her. "You look like you're being chased." He glanced behind her in obvious concern.

"Oh!" She blinked rapidly, her breath coming in gasps. "Uh, hi, Wil. No, I'm fine." She gave him a weak smile. "I guess I forgot how cold October

1

mornings can be in Montana. All that time in California must have thinned my blood." Her heart was pounding so loudly in her chest she was surprised Wil couldn't hear it.

Wil let her go. "I guess so," he said, but he didn't seem convinced. He glanced out the back door again before shutting it.

"I came in early to get some work done, but the food smells divine. Any chance I can get a couple of eggs?" Sunny asked. Her belly churned. She honestly didn't feel like eating, but asking for food was the best way to keep Wil from interrogating her. Life was hard enough at the moment. She didn't need her grandmother finding out about all the trouble she'd been having, and if Wil knew, he'd tell June and Nancy, and the whole town would know.

Wil smiled. "Let me guess, over easy with a side of fries and some tzatziki sauce?"

"How did you know?" Sunny gave a shaky laugh as she took off her coat and followed him into the kitchen. "I guess I'm pretty boring, always ordering the same thing." She opened the door to what used to be a storage pantry but was now her office. Sunny went in and hung her coat on the hook behind her desk.

For a moment, she stood, hand pressed to her chest, willing her heart to go back to its regular rhythm. It was moments like this when she missed California the most. She'd been so happy there for the last seven years. She had friends, a life, a career. She'd gone to Cornell, gotten her degree in Hospitality, and now was managing a…diner. She knew she shouldn't complain. It wasn't much of a life, but she owed Gran everything. She wasn't going to leave Gran on her own even if the town had turned against Sunny.

She grabbed her water bottle off her desk and headed into the kitchen to fill it.

Wil prepared a couple of orders of eggs and home fries, quick as always, and slid the plates on the counter of the pass-through window and hit the old-fashioned bell. June appeared, grabbed the food from the dining-room side of the window, and gave Sunny a wave. "Mornin'. You're here early." Then she disappeared again.

Wil got some fries from the freezer in the corner on the other side of Sunny's office and came back to the deep fryer. He was a big man with warm brown eyes and a shock of white hair that covered his whole head. Sunny had known him for as long as she could remember, and his hair had always been white. She had no idea how old he was since his face had always looked the same, too.

Wil whistled a vaguely familiar tune as he worked. When he turned to grab more oil for the griddle, he saw her watching him. "Monkey, you've been coming here since you were still in your mama's belly. Your order hasn't changed since you

3

discovered I could make you French fries for breakfast."

"Not true. I used to use ketchup, but now I like Tzatziki sauce. See? I have changed."

Wil laughed. "I stand corrected. You're walking on the wild side now, you and Kendra. She always orders it, too." He wiped his hands on his white apron and then grabbed a couple of eggs and cracked them on the griddle.

She watched as he buzzed around the kitchen, his moments sure and quick from years of practice. Sunny let out a long breath. She'd needed the familiarity and routine of the kitchen to bring her back to reality. It was stupid to be scared. Logically, she knew no masked men were going to jump out at her this early in the morning—in broad daylight—but tell that to her nerves.

"Here you go, Monkey." Quicker than should have been possible, Wil handed her a plate of food, made the way she liked it.

"Thanks, Wil." She took the plate back to her office, shutting the door behind her. She put the food down on her desk and all but collapsed in her chair. Head cradled in her hands, she did a few deep-breathing exercises. She needed to get her equilibrium back. This was ridiculous. She couldn't keep giving in to her fears.

After the last breath, she lifted her head and looked at her food. Her stomach growled. She tentatively picked up a fry and took a bite. It tasted like heaven. She would never have had fries in California. Breakfast had been green smoothies with fruit.

But that had been a different life. She'd come back to Canyon Springs six months ago because her grandmother was sick, and now she had to stay for a very different reason.

For a reason that might send her to prison for the rest of her life.

CHAPTER 2

Hudson Riggs planted his boot on the bottom rung of the wooden fence and leaned on his elbows. He took a sip of black coffee from his mug and smiled down at the black and white mutt lying at his feet.

It was going on a month back at the farm, but it still felt good to be home. He loved autumn mornings in Canyon Springs. The crisp fall air in his lungs, the fall blooms in their boxes, the beams of sunlight that would be shining in his eyes if not for his cowboy hat.

He'd missed it more than he'd realized. He'd been worried that the bitter taste of his father disowning him would mar his return, but now that the man had been dead two years, the bad memories had faded. It had been a sweet homecoming.

Hudson couldn't get over the change in the ranch. His father had damn near run it into the ground by the time he died. His mom was a miracle worker. She stepped in after her husband's death, and now the ranch was the most prosperous one in the area.

A gelding nickered in the field in front of him. Dancer, his mom's favorite. She'd been gone to Florida for a few weeks now, and the horse had to miss her. Hudson made a mental note to bring some carrots down to him the next time he went to the barn.

He drank the rest of his coffee, soaking in the atmosphere, then breathed out a sigh. He had a rough day ahead and no one to blame for it but himself. "Come on, Huck," he said as he turned to walk back to the house. The dog promptly got to his feet, stretched, and then took off for the porch. Hudson followed him.

His boot hit the top step of the big wrap-around porch as the side door opened with the squeak of rusty springs. "You might want to oil that," his friend Rhys said as he stepped out onto the porch. He carried a matching coffee mug in his hand, full to the brim.

"Did you make another cup for me?" Hudson asked.

"No." Rhys sat down on one of the big wooden rockers Hudson's mom had scattered around the porch. His red plaid shirt looked tight across the shoulders, but that was to be expected. He was slightly wider than Hudson, and it was Hudson's shirt.

"If that shirt rips, you owe me a new one," he commented.

"Not my fault the airline lost my luggage. You said come visit. I'm here. Anything that happens to me here is your fault." Huck leaned against Rhys's chair and nosed his hand. Rhys obliged by rubbing behind the dog's ears.

Hudson grinned. "So that's how it is? You take my stuff and my dog?"

"Yes." Rhys nodded. "That's how it is."

Hudson shook his head and walked through into the kitchen. He placed his mug beneath the new built-in coffee maker, hit the button, and held his breath.

The machine started buzzing and whirring. Hudson assumed it was going about its business. He was still trying to get used to it. His mother had it installed when she redid the kitchen. The stupid thing was intimidating with all of its bells and whistles, but it made a damn fine cup of coffee.

Hudson looked around. The house looked amazing. His mom had gone all out with new cabinetry and appliances. All top end. Everything was stainless steel. The countertops were a dark granite while the cabinets were creamy white.

It was a show kitchen as far as he was concerned, and he was terrified he was going to break something. Formica and plain old white appliances were what he was used to. This fancy-schmancy stuff stressed him out.

When the machine finished, Hudson picked up his cup of black gold and went back out to the porch to join his friend. "What are you doin' up so early?" Hudson asked as he sat down. "I figured you'd be out cold for half the day. It's a long haul from the other side of the earth." Huck left Rhys and settled at Hudson's feet.

Rhys shrugged. "I caught some shut-eye on the flight over."

"Uh-huh." Hudson eyed his friend. "How long have I known you?"

"Ten years, give or take."

Hudson nodded. "In all that time, I've never seen you catch more than twenty minutes of sleep on an airplane. Not back when it was on a military flight, and not now when it's on one of the cushy private jets that Black Thorn uses for our private security jobs."

Rhys glared at him. "Okay, jackass, you made your point. I don't like not being in control of the plane. I'll probably sleep this afternoon."

Hudson grinned. "Leg bothering you?"

Rhys's only response was to shoot him a hard look and take a long sip of his coffee.

Hudson held in a sigh. "Next topic." He cleared his

throat. "I have to go into town today. I've got a new job."

Rhys raised an eyebrow. "What? Looking after this place isn't enough for you? I thought this was supposed to be a vacation."

"It is. For you. Getting shot is no small thing. You need a chance to rest up, and recovering in the Middle East so you can avoid your family is a bad idea.

Rhys shook his head. "The last thing I want is for my five sisters to fuss over me endlessly. They'd panic and drive me crazy about my job, then treat me like I'm a kid. I don't need that," Rhys growled.

"Fair enough but you need to sit on your ass and give your leg time to heal. There's a doctor attached to the spa that specializes in traumatic injury something or other. I thought you could go see her."

Rhys shook his head. "I'm fine. I don't want to see another doctor. Besides, if we're talking about family avoidance, you'll win top prize. You haven't been back here since you left after high school. What's that, fourteen years? And how long did you wait before telling your mom that you quit the SEALs two years back to work for a private contractor?"

Hudson snorted. "That's different. My father disowned me. I couldn't come back. I met up with Mom and Hailey in Europe a few times. And anyway, Mom wants me to be happy, and I am. Well, I am, but I'm bored here. I've been on leave from work for weeks already, and if I don't do something soon, I'm gonna lose my mind.

"Don't get me wrong, I'm glad Mom is down with Hailey in Florida helping her with the pregnancy and stuff, but Mom runs a tight ship, and the ranch requires very little input from me. I can't sit around and twiddle my thumbs for the next two months 'til she gets back. The only things I could do to help, I've done. Someone's coming next week to repaint the barns and hang the new gate."

Rhys stared out at the paddock and absently rubbed his leg. "So, what's the job?"

"Personal security."

Rhys turned back to face Hudson. "Black Thorn has clients here in the U.S.?" he asked. "Josh Baker's reach is further than I thought."

"No. Not Baker." Hudson shook his head. "I called a guy I met ten years back when I first finished BUDS training. He's got his own security company going over in Eagle Rock. His name is Hank Patterson."

"And he just happens to have a job here?" Rhys gave him another hard look.

"You'd be amazed by the number of rich and famous people who hide out in these hills," Hudson said.

"Uh-huh, I'm sure. So you'll be protecting some beauty queen celebrity? You'll stand around and hold her packages and her pooch in a bag while she shops?" Rhys snorted. "I'm gonna need a picture to send to the team. They'll definitely want to see that."

Hudson frowned. "Not exactly a celebrity, no." He took a gulp of coffee and shifted in his chair.

Rhys narrowed his eyes. "Who exactly are you protecting?"

"Sunny."

Rhys raised an eyebrow. "Uh, isn't she the woman you left in the dust when you took off?"

"Yeah." Hudson grimaced. "She's the one."

"No offense, but why does she want *you* to look after her?"

"She probably doesn't," he admitted. "She's in a bit of trouble."

"What kind of trouble is she in?"

"Well…" He winced. "She allegedly killed a guy we went to high school with."

Rhys's eyebrows went sky-high. "Jesus. Are you sure you want to do this?"

"No, but there's no way Sunny's guilty. I've already started poking around, trying to figure out what happened, but I'm not getting anywhere. I've also heard rumors that Sunny's being harassed. I know I can help with that at least, but if I go to her directly and ask to help, I'm pretty sure she'd tell me to go to hell."

"What did you do?" Rhys asked in a way that telegraphed he thought the job had all the hallmarks of a bad idea.

"I called Hank and asked him for a favor. He approached Sunny's lawyer and told him he'd heard about her troubles. Hank offered help, and her lawyer said yes."

"So, you volunteered for a job—correct me if I'm wrong—you're not even getting paid for and asked a favor from a virtual stranger to make it happen so you can help Sunny. Seems like a whole lot of effort for something that's likely to go south."

Rhys frowned. "Remember, it's been a long time since high school. People change. You don't know her anymore. Don't go assuming anything about her. It'll only get you in more trouble." He shot Hudson a weighing look. "Have you seen her at all since you've been back?"

"Nope. I've, ah, sort of avoided her."

Rhys shook his head ruefully. "That's not like you. You're usually a bull-by-the-horns type of guy."

"Usually." Hudson clenched his jaw. "I was an ass to her. We had big plans. I …" He ran his hand over the back of his neck. "Well, I guess it doesn't matter now. But I'll be honest, the fact she's back here managing the local diner makes me sad. I guess this is my way of doing something for her."

"You feel guilty you left her behind," Rhys finished for him. "But everyone's in control of their own lives. What she did with hers is not on you."

Hudson took a sip of coffee. What Rhys said made sense. If only he could convince himself it was true.

"When are you meeting Sunny?"

Hudson glanced at his watch. "In a little while, I guess."

"If you're going to pretend it's a real job, just showing up seems a bit casual," Rhys said, and then he snorted. "You're going to, what, pop up in the diner? Let her know you're the guy the lawyer sent?"

Hudson nodded. "Seems like the best approach."

Rhys started to laugh. "You're afraid she's going to kick your ass, and you want lots of people around just in case. Wuss!"

"I like to think of it as being prudent," Hudson said, but he *was* wimping out. Just like he'd wimped out over the last month when he'd passed the diner a dozen times without going in.

"Prudent, my ass." Rhys hooted with laughter. "You're afraid of a girl!"

"A woman. And you're damn right." When Hudson stood, Huck instantly roused from sleep and clambered to his feet. Hudson patted the dog's head. "I should get going. You gonna be okay out here on your own?"

"I think I can handle it. Besides, I have Huck to keep me company," Rhys said, still smiling. "You gonna change into a suit and be all professional?"

Hudson glanced down at his worn jeans and navy sweater. "Nah. I think the suit might piss her off more. Besides, if I wore a suit, no one around here would take me seriously. I'm not exactly a suit kinda guy, at least as far as they know."

"She has no idea you're coming, and she has no idea you're her new security detail." Rhys burst into laughter again. "This is going to go so wrong, brother. So wrong. Better you than me."

Hudson ground his teeth. Rhys was right. He'd screwed up with Sunny years ago, and this was an even bigger mess waiting to explode in his face, but he felt compelled to help his old flame. Her memory had gotten him through more nights in the Middle East than she'd ever know. He owed her for that.

CHAPTER 3

Sunny looked, unseeing, at the drab, off-white walls of her tiny office. She missed L.A. Her office there had boasted a view of the ocean. Here, there was nothing much to look at except for a calendar of puppies from two years ago on the wall across from her, plus a sagging set of bookshelves stacked with dusty old files and paperwork.

There wasn't room for two in the office unless the door was closed, but this was what passed for heaven these days: a space to be alone and busy. Sighing, she glanced at the clock on her computer screen. It was well past noon

When she picked up her water bottle, she realized it was empty. One of the better habits she'd picked up during her time in California was staying hydrated. Water bottle in hand, she moved out from behind her desk and walked into the kitchen to refill it.

"I was coming to find you, Sunny. Someone out front wants to see you," Nancy said as she grabbed a plate off the pass-through counter, her bleach-blond beehive wobbling as she moved. Nancy had worn a beehive since she was born. Sunny was convinced of it. She and June were her grandmother's best friends since kindergarten, some seventy-odd years ago.

"Who?" she asked, but Nancy was already gone. Sunny bit her lip. She never would have worried about an unexpected visitor in the past, but now it always seemed like bad news when someone came looking for her.

She set down her empty water bottle and adjusted her dark purple blouse and black slacks. Then, squaring her shoulders, she pushed out of the kitchen into the hallway that led to the front of the restaurant. When she came around the corner, she stopped at the edge of the long counter that ran the length of the diner.

The diner was decorated in true fifties style, the same as when Jeb O'Toole, one of her grandma's best friends, had first opened it, and it had never seen a major upgrade. Round, faded leather stools lined the counter, and two rows of short booths cut down the middle. The higher booths lined the outside walls, leaving the view to the street clear. The diner was packed, as it usually was at this time of day, but no one attempted to wave her down.

She caught Nancy's eye, and the server pointed to

a booth against the far wall. Sunny nodded, already walking around the counter to the outside aisle. When Sunny looked back, Nancy was elbowing June, another server, and pointing toward the booth where Sunny was headed. June's eyebrows winged up. It was her *that's trouble* look. Sunny's belly knotted. She still couldn't see the person's face because he was holding a menu, but it was a man with brown hair.

"Can I help you?" Sunny asked as she came around the end of the booth. She stopped dead.

Hudson Riggs looked up at her for the first time in twelve years. "Hi, Sunshine."

Sunny couldn't breathe. Her heart galloped in her chest. If asked to make a list of the one hundred people who might be waiting for her in this booth, she wouldn't have written his name. She'd heard he was back in town, but he hadn't shown up and she hadn't gone looking.

"It's Sunny," she croaked. Her throat went dry. The only one who was allowed to call her Sunshine was her grandmother. Hudson had lost the right years ago.

"Sunny," he said as if he was testing it out for the first time. "How are you doin'?"

How the hell did he think she was doing? He must have heard what happened by now. He had to know what people thought of her. "Fine. I'm doing fine. And you?"

"I'm good." He gestured to the seat across the booth. "Join me?"

She wanted to turn on her heel and run, but she knew every customer in the diner would be watching at this point, and whatever she did would be reported far and wide. She sighed inwardly. "No thanks," she said with a tight smile.

She'd always hoped he'd gone bald since leaving her. Not the cool, shaved head type of bald but the *I have three strands of hair left, and I'm going to comb them over my big shiny pate* kind of bald.

But the world wasn't fair, and of course he was gorgeous, even more so than he'd been in high school. Thick strands of shiny dark brown hair curled around his ears and his collar, an errant lock flopping over his forehead. No military buzz cut for him, which sucked because now she wanted to run her fingers through it.

His blue eyes were just like she remembered them —the color of the Montana sky on a cold winter's day—and the navy sweater he wore clung to his shoulders and chest. She was pretty sure there wasn't an ounce of fat on him. Maybe she shouldn't be surprised. This was just one more nightmare to add to her list.

"Just for a coffee?"

Sunny shook her head. "No sorry, I'm busy. No time for reminiscing." She gave him a quick nod and then turned on her heel and headed back in the direction she'd come. There wasn't much she could control these days, but she could at least spare herself the indignity of a casual chat with the man who'd broken her heart so thoroughly back in high school.

She walked swiftly away, but a man suddenly stood up in a booth she was approaching and threw his meal at her. A cheeseburger platter complete with French fries hit her squarely in the chest.

"Oh!" she yelped as she stumbled. She looked up at Byron Winters, her mouth open in surprise. "What —?" Seeing the look on his face, she snapped her mouth shut. There was no point in asking. She knew full well what this was about. The burger had left a grease stain on her top, chased by a streak of ketchup and mayonnaise. It was ruined for sure.

"Dad! I can't believe you did that!" Marla Winters glared at her father. "I am *so* sorry, Sunny," she said as she stood up.

"Don't you apologize for me." Winters pointed at Sunny. "She deserved it. This is my favorite place to eat, and now she's spoiling it for me."

Hudson's voice came from over her shoulder. "Maybe you want to explain why you attacked Sunny with your lunch?"

Great. Hudson was sticking his nose in where it didn't belong.

"Byron!" June bustled up the aisle from the other direction. "What'd ya do that for?"

Winters pulled his red ball cap lower on his forehead and then pointed at Sunny. "She's a killer. She should be behind bars, not out here doing as she pleases."

"What happened to innocent 'til proven guilty?" Hudson asked.

Winters scoffed. "Everyone knows she did it. She killed Wayne."

"Dad!" Marla yelped. Her face was the color of the ketchup on Sunny's blouse.

"Well, it's true. You said so yourself."

Sunny hadn't thought it was possible for Marla's face to get any redder, but it did, somehow, deepening to a shade that reminded Sunny of an overripe plum. So Marla thought she'd killed Wayne, too. *Great*. She had thought of Marla as, well, if not a friend, then at least a friendly acquaintance.

June grabbed a rag and tried to help Sunny wipe herself off, but Sunny brushed her hands away. She knew the whole diner was watching now. She looked around, trying to make eye contact with as many people as she could, including Marla. The time had come for her to make a public statement, and this was as public as it got. Maybe some of them would take the hint and leave her the hell alone. "Mr. Winters, Marla, I can assure you I did not kill Wayne Bradley."

"I don't believe you."

"Well, Mr. Winters, that is your right, but it

doesn't change the fact I had nothing to do with his death."

Marla looked down at her plate. Not surprising. No one wanted to look Sunny in the eyes these days.

"I think you owe the lady an apology," Hudson said. He was standing directly beside Sunny now.

Her heart sunk. *No. No. No. Don't do this. You'll only make it worse.*

"Hudson, leave it," she whispered.

He ignored her warning. "And you need to pay her dry-cleaning bill."

She swore long and loud in her head. She didn't need or want Hudson to defend her. He was going to make everything worse. Couldn't he see that? She didn't care about the stains on her blouse. Yelling at Byron Winters or throwing him out would only make her the "bad guy" in the town's eyes.

"Hudson," she said from between clenched teeth, "stop."

Winters snorted. "That's right, son, you'd better quit while you can. I don't owe this *lady* nothing."

Hudson pushed in front of Sunny as he drew himself up to his full height, which had to be over six feet. He'd grown since high school. He was bigger and broader, more of a man. And he was leaning toward Winters in a way that spoke of intimidation. "I suggest you rethink that statement, Mr. Winters."

Winters blinked. As one of the town's "grumpy

old men," he was used to being left alone no matter what garbage he spewed.

June pulled at Winters's arm. "You don't want to do anything else that's gonna get you in trouble, Byron. You're gonna get kicked outta here if you don't behave."

He shrugged off June's hand. "Leave me alone, old woman. I been coming here since Elvis was King. Ain't nobody gonna throw me out." He turned back to Hudson. "You need to watch yourself, son." He pointed a thumb at Sunny. "You lie down with dogs, you're gonna get up with fleas."

Hudson's teeth clicked together, and his hands curled into fists. "You're gonna apologize to Ms. Travers and pay for her dry cleaning."

Byron tried to straighten up and puff out his chest. "Or what?"

Heat rolled up Sunny's neck and bloomed across her cheeks. "Stop, please," she hissed at Hudson as she tugged on his sweater sleeve.

Hudson didn't acknowledge she was there but shifted to completely block her.

"Or I'll have to take you down to the station and charge you with assault," a loud voice said.

Sunny turned toward the voice. Officer Colin Edwards stood in the doorway of the diner. He had on his uniform, and his hands rested on his gun belt. Relief washed over her. She let out a long breath she hadn't realized she was holding. Even though Colin had been the one to arrest her, she was willing to forgive him if it meant he could resolve this situation before it got any worse.

Winters glanced toward Officer Edwards and then back at Hudson. "You're lucky he walked in, son. I don't take kindly to having strangers get in my face."

Hudson leaned closer until they were nose to nose. "Well, then let me introduce myself. Hudson Riggs. I believe you know my mother."

Winters's mouth opened and closed like a fish looking for food. He'd likely thought Hudson a stranger passing through, not the homegrown hero who also happened to be the son of one of the most well-respected women in town.

"Dad…" Marla looked at her father as she fidgeted with a fork on the table.

Winters finally found words. "Well, now, I didn't know—"

"It doesn't change a damn thing," Hudson growled. "You still owe Sunny an apology, and you *will* pay for her dry cleaning."

Wilson frowned. "I don't think—"

"He's right, Byron. It's the only fair way to resolve this. You don't want to have to come down to the station." Officer Edwards walked up beside Sunny, nodded at her, and then gently moved her out of the way.

Colin Edwards was tall, almost the same height as

Hudson, but he wasn't nearly as broad. He was more of the tall, lanky type. He had warm brown eyes and a thick crop of red hair he kept short in a military cut. All the girls in town thought he looked good in his uniform, or at least that's what June said. Sunny had never seen his appeal, but he'd married the head cheerleader from her class, so she suspected she was alone in that.

"Thanks for the call, Miss Nancy." Colin gave her a small wave before returning his attention to the situation at hand. "Hudson," he said and nodded his head.

Hudson didn't take his eyes off Winters, but he raised his chin slightly in acknowledgement. "Colin."

"Hudson, I need you to back off a bit. Mr. Winters is going to do the right thing, aren't you Byron?" He glanced at Winters.

Winters glared at Hudson and then at Sunny. "I don't think I should have to apologize for nothin'. She killed Wayne Bradley. She should be behind bars, not out here where she could kill someone else who pisses her off."

Sunny had had enough. She didn't need to stand here and suffer further humiliation. She moved around the group gathered at the booth and made a beeline for the little hallway to the back. There was no point in trying to argue with people like Byron Winters. He had already tried and convicted her. Nothing would change that, and hearing an apology he didn't mean certainly wasn't going to make her feel better.

She pushed open the door to the kitchen. Wil gave her a sad little smile that indicated he had heard everything, or at least enough to understand the context. She grimaced and entered her office, closing the door behind her. Once in her desk chair, she closed her eyes and indulged herself again by swearing long and loud in her head. Then she opened her eyes, grabbed some tissues off her desk, and started wiping the mess off her blouse. At least it hadn't been soup or chili.

Her life had been like this since she was first arrested. People accused her of not only killing Wayne, but all kinds of unspeakable acts. She'd known most of them since she was a child, but it didn't seem to matter. They all thought she was guilty, only she wasn't, which meant the killer was still out there.

CHAPTER 4

"You need to back off, Hudson. I don't want to have to bring you down to the station, too," Officer Edwards said.

Hudson turned and glared at the cop. There wasn't a hope in hell of this guy taking him anywhere he didn't want to go. Edwards might have grown since high school, but the guy was still no match for him.

"I won't be going down to the station, Officer, but I think you should probably take him with you." He gestured with his thumb toward Winters. "He assaulted the manager of the diner and caused a scene."

Part of him wanted to stick around and ensure the officer actually did his job, but he'd seen the way Sunny had hustled back to her office. He was pretty sure she was livid at him.

Hudson made his way to the back of the diner. Nothing had gone to plan. He should have kept his cool, but the last thing he'd expected was for one of the customers to throw their food at her. Degrading didn't cover it.

Seeing Sunny had knocked him for a loop. She looked even better than his memory of her. She was still beautiful and fierce. He hated to admit, but one of the main reasons he hadn't tried to see her was because he was terrified she'd be sad and bitter like some of the other people he'd seen around town. Time did funny things to people sometimes. He couldn't have stomached it if Sunny had been beaten down somehow. He felt guilty enough as it was.

Hudson swore silently. Tensions were running high. He vowed to be by Sunny's side until this was over. Maybe he'd even call Hank and ask about getting some backup. This was turning into a real job.

He walked through the kitchen door, and Wil pointed at the office. Hudson nodded his thanks, and Wil grinned and crossed himself. Great. Sunny was furious for sure. He opened the door to her office and found her with her head in her hands.

His chest tightened. Anger he knew what to do with. Sad and a little broken? Nope, he'd never been good with that. "Sunny."

She straightened and scowled. "What did you think you were doing? I had the whole situation under control. You didn't need to stick your nose in. It made everything worse! Now they're going to think I can't speak for myself."

She had a point. Showing weakness now wouldn't help her situation at all. "You're right. I'm sorry. I kinda saw red when he threw that food at you and then started with the accusations and name calling."

Sunny stood up. "Byron Winters has always been an ass, and he's unlikely to change this late in life. You've crushed any hope of losing the title of this town's juiciest bit of gossip. The world will be talking about how you jumped to my rescue. I don't need more attention, Hudson."

He leaned against the doorjamb and ran a hand through his hair. "I am sorry."

"Great. Now please leave." Sunny sat back down.

"Um, I can't really do that." This was the moment he'd been dreading, the reason he'd procrastinated all morning about coming face to face with Sunny. She wasn't likely to take kindly to the fact the man who'd stomped all over her heart had been "hired" to protect her. But there was no way in hell he was leaving her again now.

"Hudson, please leave." Sunny glared at him. She hadn't aged a day. Well, that wasn't exactly true. She'd filled out in all the right places. He hadn't failed to notice her firm, round ass when she'd walked away from him earlier. Nor had he missed the way her blouse stretched across her chest.

Her blond hair was still shiny, and even though it was tied up in a bun, he could tell it was long and knew from experience it would be like silk in his fingers. The biggest change was in her eyes—they held a wariness that hadn't been there all those years ago.

Hudson sighed and then straightened. He moved forward and closed the office door.

"What are you doing?" Sunny demanded.

"Sunny, I can't leave. I have to stay close to you."

She shot out of her chair. "You sure as hell do *not* have to stay close to me. Now leave!" She pointed to the doorway.

Hudson didn't budge. The office was tiny, only two feet separated them. He could reach out and touch her, and he sure as hell wanted to. Which was why he jammed his hands into his front pockets. He needed to be professional.

Her scent wafted over to him. Lilacs. It brought back…memories. Memories of days gone by when it was going to be them against the world. He missed that more than he ever thought possible.

"Get out!" she spoke through clenched teeth.

The phone on her desk rang. It was the old-fashioned kind with a rotary dial. Sunny ignored it and continued to glare at Hudson.

Hudson sighed. He was going to lie to her, and it made him very sad, but he knew she'd say no if he told her the truth. He wanted to protect her. He owed her that much. Hell, he owed her more.

"Sunny, I'm sorry, but you're stuck with me. I was hired by your lawyer to protect you. Vince believes you're in danger. The town is on edge for all kinds of reasons, and you being blamed for Wayne's murder puts you in the crosshairs. After seeing what happened out there, I'm inclined to agree with him."

"Oh, for goodness' sake. That's ridiculous. I'm not in anyone's crosshairs." She rolled her eyes. "People are upset about losing Wayne. They all thought he was going to save Canyon Springs, but they'll get over it."

A small gasp escaped her mouth, and she immediately covered it with her hand. Lowering it back down slowly, she said, "I didn't mean... I *am* sorry Wayne is dead. No one should have to die like that. Alone and by another's hand.

"Vince is right. Everyone's mourning his loss, and tempers are running high at the moment. On top of everything else, there's talk of the spa closing down. The Wellness Retreat at Canyon Springs brings in a lot of revenue for the town and employs a lot of people. Plenty of people are on edge. But it has nothing to do with *me*."

"The stain on your shirt suggests otherwise," he said.

"Byron Winters is upset because his grandson's on the high school football team, and Wayne was full of big promises about getting Jackson recruited by one of the big schools. So Byron's especially pissed, and he wants someone to blame it on. Most people just ignore me or won't look me in the eye."

But he saw something in her eyes, something that told him what he already knew. There were others who'd done more than that. People who'd outright intimidated her or insulted her to her face.

"So you see, I don't need your help. I appreciate Vince thinking of me, but it's not necessary. Nor is it wanted."

Hudson folded his arms across his chest. He had to say the right thing, get Sunny to see reason. "Sunny, I hear what you're saying, and I agree there is a lot of other stuff going on in town. The thing is, with tempers running so hot, if one person's having a bad day or wants to take their rage out on someone, they're gonna look to the town scapegoat. They're gonna look to *you*. I think you need to take a step back and lay low for a while. Just until this blows over."

"Blows over." Sunny let out a harsh laugh. "What makes you think this will blow over? I was arrested for *murder* two months ago. They've stopped looking for anyone else. This is not going to blow over. This ends with me going to court and fighting for my life!" Her voice broke.

Hudson's instincts took over, and he took a small step forward, intent on wrapping his arms around her. He needed to feel her in his arms, to know she was safe, and she needed a hug. She looked so fragile standing there with tears in her eyes, worry and terror written all over her face.

Sunny moved back, hitting her chair as she swatted his arms. "What the hell do you think you're doing?"

Hudson blinked. "I…I wanted to give you a hug."

She snorted. "I don't need your hugs, and it's like I said, I can take care of myself."

There was a knock, and the door swung open, almost hitting Hudson in the ass. He whirled around to see Nancy standing there.

"Oh, sorry, hon. Didn't mean to scare you." Nancy smiled at Hudson, but he could see the twinkle in her eye.

"No problem." He smiled back.

"Sunny, Jeb called and asked me to check on you. He said he called the office, but you didn't answer. You know how quick gossip gets around in this town. He heard about the Byron Winters incident already."

"Please tell him I'm fine, Nancy. There's no need for him to fret."

Nancy laughed. "Jeb's not likely to stop worrying. He thinks of you as one of his own grandkids, but I'll tell him. He's insisting you take the rest of the day off, if not the whole week."

Sunny put her hands on her hips. "I don't need time off."

Nancy scoffed. "Of course, you don't. You're tough enough to get through anything. That's what I told Jeb. But your grandmother will have heard everything by now, and we both know she'll be in a tizzy. She's not likely to relax until she's seen you with her own eyes."

Sunny sighed, and her hands fell away from her hips. Her shoulders slumped in defeat. "You're right. I didn't think of Gran finding out. I should have called her immediately. I know you all will be fine without me, but if you need anything, please call."

"We will, hon. You have a nice afternoon with your grandmother. Tell her June and I will call her later, after *Jeopardy*'s over." Nancy looked at Hudson. "Good to see ya. It's a nice thing you're doin' for your mom. Lettin' her have time with your sister before the baby comes. Don't be a stranger." She tapped him on the arm and then turned on her heel and disappeared.

Hudson turned back toward Sunny, but she shot him a warning look. "Don't say a word. I'm going home, but only because it will make Jeb and my grandmother feel better."

Hudson knew not to open his mouth. He backed out of the office as she grabbed her purse from the desk drawer and her jacket off the hook behind her desk. Holding out a hand, he signaled she should precede him, and she huffed past.

"You can follow me home in your car, but once we're there, you're done," she said, her tone hard. "The only reason I'm letting you follow me is because I can't stop you. Do you hear me? When I'm home, you're gone."

That wasn't going to happen, but this wasn't the time or place to have that argument. He was hoping once he got in the house, Clara would back him up. She'd always liked him. Well, she'd always liked him *before* he had broken her granddaughter's heart. Who knew how she felt now?

Sunny went out the back door to the parking lot and started walking toward the far corner. There was a silver BMW convertible parked there, nose in, next to June's ancient pickup. *Sunny's?* The roof was up because it was October, but Hudson had no problem imagining Sunny driving around town with the roof down as soon as it was warm enough. She'd always loved driving with the windows down when they were together.

How could she afford a BMW on a diner manager's salary? *Was there an ex-husband?* His hands started to curl into fists, so he cracked his knuckles instead.

He'd tried to find her on social media once, but she'd kept her accounts private, and he didn't think she'd say yes to a friend request.

A couple years after he'd left, his mom had said

Sunny was back for a visit from college and brought a boyfriend with her. It was serious, or so she'd thought. Hudson damn near threw up at the news. Any news about Sunny was strictly forbidden after that. He didn't want to hear it.

They were the only two souls in the parking lot— Hudson practically had a sixth sense for who was around him, and he'd taken a quick look to back it up —so he'd let her walk ahead. She needed to let off a little steam, and he wanted to give her space so she could come around to the idea he was going to be protecting her. Plus, it gave him a chance to admire her ass some more. And it was an ass that deserved to be admired.

Sunny walked around to the driver side of the car and stopped dead. Her body went rigid. Hudson was beside her in a flash.

Someone had scrawled *KILLER!* across the driver's side of the car in what looked like red spray paint.

"Son of a bitch," he murmured. He scoped out the parking lot again, but they were still alone. Sunny was swaying a bit so he put an arm around her shoulders to steady her.

She immediately stiffened and moved away. "I'm fine," she muttered. She opened her purse and pulled out her keys.

"You can't drive it, Sunny."

"Why not? How else am I going to get home?"

"I'll take you."

"No—"

"You don't have a choice, Sunny. Unless you want the cops to take you home."

She shuddered. "No." Her voice was barely a whisper. "I don't want to call the cops."

Hudson fisted his hands. He wanted to kill whoever had done this. Sunny was exhausted and sad. It was obvious she wanted to keep a low profile. She clearly didn't trust the police, and while he couldn't blame her, he had to make her see reason.

"You have to call them. You're gonna want a police report for your insurance."

She frowned but seemed unconvinced.

Hudson played his ace in the hole. "This will upset your grandmother, too. You don't need her to see this."

Sunny looked up at him for the first time since they'd hit the parking lot. She bit her lip and then nodded. She followed him to his pickup and said nothing as he boosted her up to the passenger seat. He moved a few steps away, intent on calling the department, but then remembered Edwards. Or, more precisely, he remembered the officer had defended Sunny when push came to shove. So he pocketed his cell phone and approached the back door of the diner. "Hey, Wil?"

Wil poked his head around the corner. "Yeah?"

"Is Edwards still there?"

Wil shook his head. "He left a couple of minutes ago."

"Shit. Do you know who would have his cell number?"

"Nancy."

"I should've known," Hudson said with a grin. Nancy had been the queen bee of town gossip when he was a kid and, apparently, nothing had changed. "Can you ask her to text it to me?" He rattled off his number.

Wil grabbed an order paper out of his pocket, jotted it down, and disappeared. Hudson closed the door and went back and stood by the car. His phone vibrated seconds later. Nancy had sent him the number and, to his surprise, she hadn't asked why he needed it. He suspected the follow-up questions would come later. If not to him, she'd grill Edwards for sure. You didn't get to be known as the gossip queen of Canyon Springs for your discretion.

He texted Edwards about the car and received a near-instant response: *Coming*. But Hudson wasn't the sort who liked to sit around while he waited, so he spent the next few minutes seeing if there was any other damage or anything left behind to identify who'd done the defacing. If there was, he didn't see it.

Two minutes later, Edwards pulled into the parking lot. Hudson was relieved Edwards was using his head. No lights and sirens. If Hudson had dialed 911, more than one cop car would have shown up with lights blazing and sirens blaring, none of which would have helped Sunny.

He glanced over at her hunkered low in the seat of his mom's new GMC Sierra Denali pickup truck. The last thing she needed at the moment was more drama. He decided right there he'd put a smile back on Sunny's face no matter what it took, and he had some pretty fantastic ideas on how he'd like to do it, too.

CHAPTER 5

Sunny slid down in the seat. She sincerely didn't want to talk to Colin Edwards again, but Hudson had a point. It wasn't like she could afford to pay for the new paint job out of pocket. She had to save every penny for her trial. Bail had cost her dearly, and she wasn't getting it back no matter what happened. The ten percent was gone forever. They never put that in cop shows.

Drawing in a shaky breath, she flexed her fingers. She needed a cup of tea or a shot of whiskey to get her hands to stop shaking. Preferably the whiskey. She closed her eyes. Actually, might as well dream big. What she really wanted was to be on her favorite rooftop patio, drinking bottomless mimosas with her best friend, Langley. She let out a big sigh. She was so far removed, it felt like L.A. had been an entirely different life. In a way, it had been.

She looked over as Edwards got out of his cruiser and approached Hudson. They stood there talking as they studied the damage to her car. Her baby. It was the first big purchase she'd ever made—a dream come true. Now she was living in a nightmare. She shivered and wrapped her jacket more tightly around herself. It was cold in the truck, and now that she was outside of the diner, she just wanted to go home. What was taking so long? Couldn't Hudson hand things over to the cop?

Seeing Edwards brought back memories of her arrest. It didn't matter that he'd been kind or that he continued to be kind. It had been a humiliating and terrifying Experience.

Hudson finally walked over and climbed into the truck, shutting the door behind him. "How you doin'?"

Sunny nodded, not feeling up to choking out a happy lie.

"Colin is gonna take pictures and fill out a report. He'll call Sandy over at the garage to come get it. Sandy will call you once he's had a look."

"Thanks," she murmured.

"No problem." Hudson started the truck and drove out of the parking lot, taking the back way out of town. Something she greatly appreciated. The fewer people who saw them together, the better. Tongues would already be wagging. Of course, that wasn't all that unusual at this point. Tongues hadn't stopped wagging since her arrest.

Hudson turned up the heat. "I don't remember it being this cold this early."

Usually, Sunny enjoyed the drive out of town to her gran's farm. She loved the idea of leaving all the people behind and ascending into the hills. It wasn't a long drive, but with Hudson sitting beside her, the drive seemed interminable.

His scent wafted over to her. Citrus still, but something more, something spicy that made her think of sex. Heat crept up her neck. Dear God, what the hell was wrong with her? She needed to get a hold of herself. "Nice truck," she blurted out. "The seats are very cushy, and it isn't nearly as bouncy as Gran's. Of course, Gran's is ancient but still, this doesn't feel like a work truck at all."

She felt the weight of Hudson's glance. She probably sounded like a rambling lunatic. Truth was, the day's happenings had thrown her for a loop. First the burger and then her car. And Hudson, of course.

"Thanks. I bought it for my mom. She hasn't had a new truck in years. I thought she might like a bit more comfort. So…can you think of anyone who is particularly upset about Wayne's death?" Hudson glanced her way quickly before returning his gaze to the road.

"The whole damn town." She frowned and swallowed the logjam of tears forming in her throat.

"Anyone specific come to mind?"

"No. People have been avoiding me and not looking me in the eye. They even call me names, but I...I guess I can't get my head around it. I've known these people for years." She shrugged, trying not to show how much it hurt her but knowing he probably saw it anyway. "The fact they think I hurt Wayne is mind-blowing." She tucked an errant hair behind her ear.

"People are scared. It's hard to believe someone they know was murdered." Hudson drummed his fingers on his steering wheel. "It's easier to believe you did it than to deal with the fact the murderer is still out there. Would you be able to sleep at night knowing there was a murderer at large?"

"I'd sleep a hell of a lot better than I do now!"

Hudson grimaced. "I didn't mean... What I'm trying to point out is people want someone to blame so they can feel better, safer. The cops arrested you, so you're bearing the brunt of their collective anger. I don't think everyone in town hates you or believes you did it, but there's a group of people who are either very frightened by what happened to Wayne or lost something because of his death. They're using you as their scapegoat."

Sunny rolled her eyes, annoyed. She'd forgotten what a know-it-all he could be. "Did you go off and do a psychology degree while you were overseas?"

Hudson's jaw tightened. "You'd be surprised what you learn about people during war time."

Guilt washed over her. She'd forgotten he'd been off fighting in a war. She sighed. "Well, if you think they're just lashing out, then there's no need for you to stay with me. I don't need protection."

"That's not what I'm saying. Desperate, frightened people can be dangerous. Today shows people in this town are not afraid to take their anger out on you. Your lawyer was right. You need protection."

Sunny remained silent. She didn't agree with Hudson or her lawyer, but at the moment she didn't have the energy to put up a fight. She'd argue with Hudson once they got to her grandmother's. Gran would back her up. She'd raised Sunny to stand on her own two feet.

Hudson signaled and pulled into her grandmother's driveway. Gran was standing on the little front porch. The look of fear on her face broke Sunny's heart. Her parents had died in a car accident when she was a small child, and her grandmother brought her home and raised her, but all Sunny had done was bring trouble to the woman's door. She swallowed hard and rubbed her eyes. Crying wouldn't help the situation.

As soon as the truck rolled to a stop, Sunny hopped out and ran up the steps threw herself into her grandmother's arms. Gran squeezed her tightly. Feeling her grandmother's trembling body released something in Sunny. Some of the tears escaped and ran down her cheeks. "I'm okay," she whispered and tried to keep the hitch out of her voice.

"Well, I know that," Gran said. "I'd expect nothing less." But she still didn't let go of Sunny. Finally, a minute or so later, Gran eased her grip on Sunny, and let her step back. Gran wiped her eyes, and Sunny's heart broke all over again. But Hudson was here so she couldn't let herself become a sobbing mess. She took a deep breath and wiped the liquid from her own cheeks, steeling herself to deal with the situation.

"Well, well. Look what the cat dragged in," Gran said.

"Ms. Clara." Hudson dipped his chin in greeting. He'd come around to stand in front of his mom's pickup.

Gran glared at him. "I was wondering when I'd see your sorry butt again. You've been in town for a good few weeks. Why haven't you come by before this?"

Oh, God. This was the last thing Sunny needed. Watching a confrontation between Hudson and her grandmother was up there with getting a root canal. "It's fine, Gran. Hudson isn't going to stick around. He gave me a ride because my car...wasn't working, and he happened to be in the parking lot at the right time. It's all good."

She turned to Hudson. "Thanks for the ride. Say

hi to your sister and mom for me." She gave him a small wave, hopefully giving him no choice but to leave., She then put an arm around her grandmother and turned to go into the little house.

Hudson cleared his throat. "Um, I can't leave. It's like I told you earlier, Sunny. I'm here to do a job."

Gran turned back to face Hudson, her gaze sharpening. "What job?"

"I'm supposed to protect your granddaughter."

"And as *I* told *you*, it's not necessary." Sunny glared at Hudson, but her whole body felt tense and on alert. "You need to leave."

Gran looked back and forth between the two. "Would one of you please fill me in? What's going on?"

Hudson leaned his butt on the bumper of the Denali. "I was hired—"

"It's silly," Sunny said, "and overly cautious. I'll call Vince and straighten it all out." She smiled at her grandmother. "Honestly, I'm fine. Hudson can go." She needed him to go so she could let her guard down. So she could talk to her grandmother without him there, watching and listening. She wouldn't let herself be vulnerable in front of Hudson. Not again.

Gran frowned. "I'd like to hear what Hudson has to say."

Sunny shot Hudson a dirty look, but he ignored it and kept his focus on her grandmother. "Sunny's lawyer, Vince, hired me to protect your granddaugh-

46

ter. I don't know how much she's told you, but she's been having some problems since she was arrested."

Gran looked at her intently, as if trying to see into her soul—something she very well might be able to do—and said, "Well, she hasn't said much, but I know people in town are giving her a wide berth. Linda over at the Quick Mart gave *me* the cold shoulder the other day, and I used to change her diapers when her mother and I worked together over at Canyon Springs Hospital. I have to figure they're being much worse to my girl here."

Sunny closed her eyes. Her stomach roiled at the thought people were being mean to her grandmother over this. As a former nurse in the maternity ward, her grandmother had helped half of the town come into this world. She opened her eyes and squeezed her grandmother's shoulder. "I'm sorry, Gran."

"Vince mentioned the cold-shoulder treatment, but he also told me about a few more serious incidents." Hudson glanced at Sunny. "Apparently, when Sunny left work last night, four masked men jumped out at her. One of them even shoved her."

Sunny bit her lip. A shiver went down her spine. When the masked men had jumped out at her, she damn near died. Her knees had given out and she'd dropped everything she was carrying. After they ran off, it took her ten minutes to calm down enough to drive home.

"After that incident, Vince thought it might be

better if Sunny had someone around to keep an eye on her. He doesn't want her to get hurt. People have a way of acting before they think."

"That's certainly true." Gran shifted her narrow-eyed gaze to Sunny. "You didn't say anything."

"Neither did you," she pointed out. "But you don't need to worry. Jeb offered to give me the rest of the week off, and I'm going to take him up on it. I won't have any more run-ins for a while." She'd said it impulsively—she hadn't planned on missing work—but the immediate sense of relief she felt, on a physical level, suggested it was a good idea.

"Well, that was nice of Jeb, and I'm glad we'll get to spend more time together." She reached for Sunny's hand and squeezed. "We can work on cleaning out the attic."

Sunny groaned. Not what she'd had in mind for her staycation. Of course, none of this was what she had in mind. "Sure, I guess. If it makes you happy."

Gran smiled. "Now Hudson, why don't you stay for dinner? Sunny can cook us something, and you can tell me all about your sister and your mom."

Sunny's smile faded. Any hope she'd had of a quiet night with her grandmother just died. Hudson in her space was the absolute last thing she needed, but she had to admit Hudson wasn't last on the list of things she wanted. He was nowhere near the bottom and way too close to the top for comfort.

CHAPTER 6

HUDSON IGNORED the daggers Sunny was shooting his way. "I'd love to stay for dinner, Ms. Clara." He got up off the bumper and followed the ladies into the house.

Sunny would just have to hate him. He fully intended to look after her. He refused to let anything else hurt her. Even without knowing the details, he was one-hundred-percent sure she was innocent. It was obvious from the way she'd reacted to Byron earlier, from the look in her eyes as she proclaimed her innocence. And from the way she'd fought, yet failed to suppress, those tears.

He wiped his boots on the welcome mat, taking his time about it, and listened to Sunny hissing at Clara as they continued into the kitchen. He'd give her a minute to get it out of her system before he followed them in. It would allow him to scout out his surroundings, look for any weaknesses a prowler could exploit.

The little house hadn't changed a bit since his high school days. The stairs across from the doorway had the same flower-patterned runner, and the blue-and-white wool afghan hanging over the back of the old brown couch in the parlor was the very one he and Sunny had curled up beneath to watch TV and do other things.

Those were fun times. Sunny was his first love, and he was hers. They were each other's first in all kinds of ways. He'd thought she was the one he'd spend forever with. And then he left her behind. He touched the afghan. He'd love to have that kind of fun with her again, but somehow he doubted she'd agree.

All the furnishings in the parlor were the same except for the brand-new flat screen TV that hung on the wall opposite the couch. Sunny must have insisted. From what he remembered, Clara wasn't too keen on change.

He walked in farther, drawn in by the old memories. Ms. Clara had the same pictures on the mantel— one of Sunny as a child, another of her parents, and then there was a picture from Clara's wedding to Sunny's grandfather. But there was one he hadn't seen before: Sunny's high school graduation photo. She looked happy, radiant even. Hudson picked it up.

His memories of her, of her hair that smelled of

lilacs, the way she fit so perfectly in the crook of his arm, and her unwavering loyalty to him, had kept him going through some long nights in Iraq and Afghanistan. He doubted she'd believe that, but it was true.

There were more photographs that were new to him. Another graduation, must be from college. He didn't know which one—he'd have to ask her about that—and a picture of Sunny next to her BMW. He couldn't place where it had been taken, the auto dealer in the background wasn't familiar. She must have gone over to Missoula to get it. He set the picture frame back on the mantel and walked back toward the front door.

The dining room, on the opposite side of the stairs, hadn't changed much either. The same long wooden table hulked in the middle, surrounded by ten matching chairs. A vase of dying wildflowers sat on the runner. Hudson moved around the stairs and made his way to the kitchen, which ran along the back of the house.

"I still don't see—" Sunny stopped speaking when she saw him standing in the entryway to the kitchen.

"Come in and sit down." Clara gestured toward the chair across from her at the small kitchen table. "Sunny is making us some chicken and a salad for dinner. Would you like something to drink? Sunny, get Hudson a beer. I think there's one left in the fridge."

"I'm fine, Ms. Clara. I don't need a beer," Hudson said as he sat down.

"Nonsense. I'm sure you'd like a beer. I know I would."

"You're not supposed to drink on your meds, Gran. You know that," Sunny admonished as she pulled open the fridge door and rummaged around. "Besides, I don't see any beer."

"There's a six-pack in the shed fridge," Clara said. "Can you go run out there and bring a few in?"

Hudson shifted in his chair, trying to get comfortable. "Sunny doesn't need to go to all that trouble for me. Water would be fine."

Sunny grabbed a glass out of the cupboard and started toward the sink.

"Well," Ms. Clara said, "I'd like a beer, and since you scared me half to death with that Byron Winters business, I think I deserve it."

Sunny's eyes narrowed on her grandmother. "Fine, but only half of one." She glanced down. "I'm going to go change, and then I'll get you the beer." She turned and went down the little hallway, and then Hudson heard her footsteps on the stairs.

He stood up. "I can go out to the shed, Ms. Clara. No need to trouble Sunny."

Clara pointed to the chair. "Don't even think about it. Park your butt in that chair again and tell me what the hell is going on."

Hudson blinked and sat back down. "Er, I'm not sure what you mean."

"Don't bullshit me, Hudson. I got half a dozen phone calls before y'all showed up. Why did Colin Edwards come back to the diner?" Clara was glaring at him with a fierce expression on her face. This was the Clara Elliott half the people in town rightly feared. This was the woman who'd singlehandedly taken on a biker gang in the ER and had them all *yes ma'aming* her in minutes.

Hudson grinned. "You're still hard-core, Ms. Clara." She hadn't lost the "fire in her belly," as his long-dead grandpa used to say.

Clara pointed her gnarled finger at him. "Don't you forget it! Now spill."

Hudson's smile died. "Someone spray painted *Killer* across the driver's side of her BMW. I got Colin to come back to make the report. Sandy has it at the garage now."

Clara nodded. "I see. Did Vince tell you everything that's been happening to her?"

Hudson hesitated. "He did. We had a call earlier today."

"Good. So you know it's a lot more than rudeness and gossip. She's been attacked at least once, and she got thrown out of the nail salon because her 'presence' caused a disturbance. I'm worried next time it won't just be a cheeseburger platter thrown at her."

"Wait, how do you know about all this?" Hudson asked. There was no way Sunny had told her.

"I might be old, but I'm not stupid. Very little happens around here without me knowing about it. Wayne wasn't back in town for long, maybe a few months, but he was full of big promises. Without him, people are afraid this town'll dry up like a creek in a drought. They're out for blood."

Hudson nodded. "Do you know anything about Wayne's murder?"

Clara shook her head. "I was having one of my spells that night, so I took a pill and it knocked me out." She sighed. "I'm having some heart issues. The old ticker isn't behaving these days. Once I take a pill, I have to sleep. I can't give Sunny an alibi because I have no idea what time she got home."

Hudson frowned. "The chief must have some serious evidence if he arrested and charged Sunny. Vince said something about a scarf?"

"Yes Sunny's scarf was used to strangle Wayne, and she delivered food to him the evening it happened. No one has admitted to seeing him alive after she did. There's also something about the food she brought over that has the chief all hot and bothered. Or so the gossip goes."

Clara sighed. "The thing is, Wayne was not the person everyone here believed him to be. There was a whole other side to him. For instance, the chief doesn't want anyone to know this, but Wayne was high as a kite the night he was killed. Supposedly that's why they think Sunny could've done it. He wouldn't be able to fight back like he normally would've. We need to dig into his business if we're going to figure out who killed him."

Hudson sighed inwardly. He didn't want to tell Clara what he was up to but, knowing her, she wasn't going to leave it alone. "Look, I've already started poking around, but it's an official police investigation. I have to tread carefully. The chief—"

Clara scoffed. "I knew Chief Wells when he was in short pants, and he was none too smart then. Time has not improved things."

She reached across the table and grabbed Hudson's hand. "Look, I don't know what happened in high school that made you skedaddle, although I have my suspicions. Your father was a hard man. Your mama is tough and put up with him all those years, but it cost her. I expect she didn't want it to cost you the same way. She's done wonders with the ranch since he passed. I think she did it to spite him."

Clara smiled. "Whatever happened, it's all water under the bridge as far as I'm concerned. I didn't know Vince was going to hire you. He said it was somebody from over Eagle Rock way, but I'm glad it's you. You know Sunny, and from what I've heard, you know what you're doing when it comes to security." She gave him an assessing look. "I heard you were a Navy SEAL and you're doing something similar now."

Hudson nodded. "Yes ma'am. I was a SEAL for about seven years. I got out of the Navy, and now I'm with a company that provides security and...other services for high-ranking executives in the middle east and other locations."

"Good. I need you to keep my girl safe. She's all I have left in this world." She squeezed his hand.

Hudson squeezed back, feeling a little choked up. After everything he'd done, she actually *trusted* him. He only hoped he could convince Sunny to trust him again, too. "I will do my best, Ms. Clara, I promise." And he meant it from the bottom of his soul. "But I need you to help me get her on board with the whole security thing."

Clara grimaced. "I'll do what I can, but you can't blame her. You cut and ran with only a short note to say you were sorry. Sunny hasn't ever forgiven you."

Hudson heard Sunny's tread on the stairs. Clara must have as well because she withdrew her hand.

Sunny came into the kitchen, wearing faded jeans and a white tank top with a black sweater that had a wide neck. The sweater slid down over her right shoulder, and Hudson swallowed hard. She looked so damn fine, her skin as lush and inviting as it had ever been. His hands ached to take her hair down and run his fingers through it. He put them in his lap in case he started to reach out.

"I'll be back in a second with the beer," Sunny stated as she walked toward the back door.

Clara frowned. "You know, I'm not sure there is any, come to think of it. I guess water will have to do, Hudson." She let out a big sigh. "One of the problems of getting old. I'm always forgetting things."

Hudson doubted Clara ever forgot a thing, and by the expression on Sunny's face as she turned away from the door, she wasn't buying it either.

"Hudson and I did have a chance to catch up a bit. He was telling me about his mom's new hobby. Seems his sister's mother-in-law, Fran, convinced her to give pickleball a try. They're in a tournament next week. Isn't that something?"

How Clara knew everything was beyond him. If the US Intelligence Service employed the people of Canyon Springs, they'd never be in the dark about anything.

"It's something all right," Sunny muttered as she launched into dinner prep.

Clara winked at Hudson, and he couldn't help but grin. This old gal was full of surprises.

"Sunny, why don't you sit a second?" Clara said and patted the chair next to her. "I think you need to fill Hudson in on what happened with Wayne Bradley."

Sunny froze. She studied her grandmother with narrowed eyes. "Why does Hudson need to know about Wayne?"

"Well, if he's going to protect you, he should know what he's up against. It's not fair to keep him in the dark."

Sunny grimaced. "Hudson's not going to protect me. I don't need protecting."

"Humor me." Clara said in a tone that made Hudson want to spill his guts, even though he wasn't the one who'd she'd been addressing.

Fine." Sunny pulled out the chair and sat down. "What do you want to know?"

Hudson cleared his throat. "Um, why don't you take me through your history with Wayne and then tell me what happened on the day of his death."

Sunny sighed and folded her hands on the table. "Wayne and I dated briefly in high school. It was in the middle of my senior year."

Guilt washed through Hudson. She didn't say it, but he heard *after you left*. He gripped the edge of the table, his mind running through the events that had led to him leaving town. Getting stuck over the thought of her dating Wayne, he silently counted to ten and tried to refocus. "So, why did you two break up?"

She shrugged. "After his first season as starting quarterback, all the girls were throwing themselves at him. I guess he didn't want to be tied down." She glanced at her grandmother. Clara's lips had flattened into a tight line. Something was going on for sure, some underlying current of conversation between grandmother and granddaughter, but he knew he wasn't going to get more out of them at the moment.

"Okay, so then what?"

"Then nothing. High school was over, and Wayne went to play for a big college out east, and then he played for the NFL briefly."

"Why did he come back?" Hudson asked. He'd skimmed some articles on Google earlier, but he wanted to hear the story from Sunny.

She shrugged. "He had a knee injury, and after that, he did some TV stuff and public speaking. I don't know why he came back to Canyon Springs. I didn't follow his career or anything."

"Your grandmother said he was only in town for a few months?"

"Yeah, he hit town a bit after I did, around the Fourth of July. The whole town was excited he was here. The mayor gave him a key to the city and had him ride on his own float in the Independence Day parade.

"It was all over the local paper he pledged to stay in town and develop a better high school sports program. There were all kinds of rumors. I heard he was going to open some sort of sports bar and restaurant and bring in a few celebrity friends."

Clara added, "Yes, and I also heard he was going to open a sporting goods store. I know Cal Chadwick was all in a tizzy about that. His family's been running Canyon Springs Sporting Goods for years."

"Yes, I heard that, too," Sunny said. Turning to Hudson, she added, "Wayne was all anyone talked about for a while."

Hudson frowned. "Did you see him or speak to him once he got back?"

Sunny shifted in her seat. "I saw him at the diner a few times. We exchanged hellos and some chit-chat, the usual stuff."

Hudson's gut tightened even more. He felt it again, the sense she was holding something back. "Did you go out with him or anything?"

"No," Sunny said immediately, but Clara gave her a pointed look. "Okay, we bumped into each other at the Green Bean Roastery one day. I was drinking coffee and catching up on emails, and he sat down and joined me."

Hudson frowned. He didn't like the idea of Wayne being near Sunny. As he remembered it, Wayne Bradley had been an asshole back in high school. "What did you talk about?"

She sighed. "He talked about helping out at the high school and doing other things around town. He wasn't specific about anything other than his work with the high school." Sunny bit her lip. "He also asked me out for dinner in Missoula. He said he was looking at a couple of restaurants to maybe invest in over there, and he wanted me to check them out with him, but I turned him down. That was the end of the conversation. I left."

Hudson had watched Sunny closely the whole time she was speaking. She was definitely not telling the whole story; it was practically written across her face. It only made him more certain she was innocent but the situation was clearly more complex than she was letting on. Still, she'd need to work on a better poker face before she got to trial, or no one would believe her. "So, what happened on the day of Wayne's death?"

Sunny let out a long sigh. "Wayne had taken a liking to the new salads on our menu at the diner. He ordered take-away from us a few times a week.

"That afternoon he called and asked to speak to me. He wanted to make a big order of food, a large salad with extra shrimp and a cheeseburger platter, but he insisted he couldn't pick it up because he had a meeting. He was wondering if I could drop it off instead." She paused and licked her lips. "It was almost six, and I was wrapping up for the day. Wayne's place was kind of on my way, so I said yes. It's my biggest regret."

Hudson waited for her to continue. He knew Sunny was going over things in her mind, deciding what to say. This was obviously difficult for her, and part of him wanted to reach out and touch her, but he knew she'd pull back if he tried. It wasn't his right to touch her anymore, and he'd do well to remember that.

"I drove over to Wayne's place. He was renting a house over by the country club in the ritzy section of town. Not sure if you've been there. It was all built after you left.

"Anyway, I buzzed the gate, and he let me in. I dropped off the food, and then I drove home." She glanced at her grandmother. "When I got home, Gran was already up in bed. She hadn't been feeling well earlier. I checked on her, but she was sleeping. I did some work, and then I went to bed. That's it. End of story."

Hudson looked between Sunny and her grandmother, taking note of Clara's pursed lips. "So why do I get the feeling there's more to it?"

Clara cleared her throat. "Well, that's 'cause there is. Wayne asked Sunny out every time he came to the diner. Lots of people heard him, and they all heard her shoot him down. Every. Single. Time. I don't think he liked that much."

Hudson glanced at Sunny. "Is that true?"

She nodded. "Yes, he asked me out a few times, but I said no."

"So how did your scarf end up around his neck?"

"When he buzzed me through the gates, he said he was out by the pool and asked if I could bring the food to him there. So I did. He was sitting at the outdoor dining table, using his phone. I left pretty quickly, but my silk scarf must have slipped off when I set the bag down. I don't know what happened to it after that. And if someone else ate some of the food, it wasn't me."

She was lying about something, which meant she, at least, didn't trust him. He couldn't blame her, but it didn't make it any less painful. "Sunny," Hudson started, "I think there's more to the story, and if *I* think there's more, then the people on the jury will think so, too. I get that you might not want to tell me, but make sure you tell Vince. He's going to need to know everything if he's going to launch the best defense possible."

Sunny glared at Hudson but said nothing.

"How did you manage to get out on bail?" Hudson asked. He'd been wondering for a while. People in town weren't necessarily too pleased about it.

"Vince argued that I was home to look after Gran, and I couldn't take off and leave her." She smiled at her grandmother. "I think it helped that Gran and the judge go way back."

Clara smiled, too. "Indeed, we do. We used to date before I met your grandfather."

Sunny sighed. "He set a high bail, but I had some money saved so I could pay it." She frowned. "Paying for the trial will be much harder."

Hudson knew because he'd looked it up. Murder trials were damn expensive, but he had money. Personal security in global hotspots paid well. He didn't offer to pay because he knew she'd refuse, but if they couldn't figure out who did this, he'd convince Clara to take his money. He could always make more.

"Now," Clara said conversationally, "tell me more about your mother's other new hobby. I hear she's playing poker, too."

CHAPTER 7

Pickleball and poker, my ass. Sunny tried not to slam the dishes on the counter, but it was damn hard. She had no idea why the hell her grandmother was so buddy-buddy with Hudson. After a lifetime of being raised by Clara Elliott, however, she knew when she was being dismissed.

Like being sent off on a wild goose chase to the shed to look for beer that didn't exist. She'd decided right then and there, she'd change first so she could listen to their conversation from upstairs, but they'd talked too softly. Well, she wasn't going to be rail-roaded into accepting Hudson's help. She'd learned long ago that trusting him wasn't the smartest course of action.

"Dinner was delicious. Why don't you let me help you wash up?" Hudson rose from the small kitchen table.

Sunny turned and glared. "Why don't you and Gran go sit in the other room and continue to catch up? Seems to me you had plenty to talk about earlier." She gave him a big fake smile.

Hudson blinked. "Um, sure."

"That sounds like a good idea," Gran said gamely, standing from the table. "Hudson, why don't we do a quick tour of the place? There are a few things that I'd like your opinion on. I hear you're fixing up your mom's place real nice." She headed for the back door before he could answer, and he followed her out.

Sunny breathed a sigh of relief. It was nice to have the small kitchen to herself. Hudson was so big his presence seemed to have overtaken the little house. It had clearly been too long since her last boyfriend because she'd been having all kinds of sexy thoughts over dinner. Remembering what it was like to be with him. Thinking about how it might be different now that he'd bulked up. She leaned over to open the window above the sink to cool her heated cheeks. She needed the cold air. Just like she needed to steer clear of Hudson Riggs and his fine ass.

She was sure Gran would take Hudson to see everything that needed sprucing up around the little farm. Before long, she'd have him volunteering to fix it. Gran could charm the birds out of the trees.

Which meant he might be around more.

"Oh, shit." She put the pot she'd been cleaning back into the sink and started toward the back door.

But what would she say to them? That she suddenly needed help in the kitchen?

If she did that, he'd be in here next to her, a foot or less away, and she wasn't so sure she could handle that. Not right now, when her will to stay away from him was so weak. She returned to the pot in the sink.

Thirty minutes later, the kitchen was clean and sparkling again, but Gran and Hudson still weren't back. It was just past twilight, but the dark had never frightened her grandmother. In all likelihood, she'd probably asked Hudson to look over the back fence. Sunny had told her it needed to be completely replaced, but her grandmother thought they could get away with replacing a few of the sections.

She made another pot of tea, poured herself a cup, and headed for the stairs. They'd come back to find an empty kitchen, and hopefully Hudson wouldn't be bold enough to attempt to come up to her room.

She was halfway up the stairs when the sound of shattering glass filled the air. Sunny screamed and dropped her mug of tea. The hot spray of liquid stung her arm, and she tripped. Her hand caught her fall, but a shard from the broken mug sliced into her palm. Cursing, she clutched onto the bannister, her grip slick from tea and blood.

It was hard to move at first—her knees refused to cooperate—but she finally started moving down the steps. She reached the bottom and flicked on the foyer light just as Hudson burst into the hall.

"Ah!" Sunny yelled again, startled. She hadn't heard him coming over the sound of her heart beating in her ears.

"Are you okay?" Hudson growled. He grabbed her by the arms as his eyes roamed over her and then the area around her.

"F-fine." She cleared her throat and tried again. "Someone smashed the parlor window," she said, even though he clearly knew. She still hadn't let go of the banister, nor did she intend to. She might fall right onto Hudson's chest if she didn't have something to grip, and she had no intention of letting him know how much this had scared her.

Sunny looked around. "Where's Gran?" True panic started to claw its way up her throat again. "Is she okay?"

"She's fine. She's in the old barn office with a shotgun."

Sunny nodded. She was too choked up to speak. If anything happened to that woman... Well, Sunny couldn't bear to think about it.

Hudson dropped his hold of her and headed into the parlor. Sunny felt the immediate loss of his warmth. Her knees started to buckle, but she pulled herself upright.

It couldn't have been more than a second or two before he came back. "You're hurt." He picked up her hand and examined it.

Sunny tried to pull away. "It's nothing. The sound

startled me, and I dropped my tea on the stairs. Then I tripped and landed on the broken china."

Hudson wouldn't let go of her hand. He looked around, presumably for something to wipe away the blood.

"I'll wash it in the bathroom," Sunny said, giving her hand another tug. This time Hudson took the hint. Even if a part of her wanted to grab on to him tight and not let go. She turned and stumbled to the little half bath under the stairs. After flicking on the light, she grabbed the white hand towel off the rack. Once she'd rinsed the cut and wrapped the towel around her hand, she went back out.

Hudson was stuffing his phone into his pocket. "I called Colin. He's on his way. I also called Clara on the barn phone to let her know you're okay." He glanced at her wrapped hand.

"It's fine." Sunny moved around him to walk into the parlor. Glass covered the old sofa and carpet, and jagged pieces were scattered across the coffee table.

He grabbed her arm. "Don't touch anything."

She nodded. "I know. I just want to see."

Hudson sighed. "It was a rock. Someone threw a rock through your window."

Her window, sure, but it was also Gran's window. Sunny slammed her bad hand against the door jam and then cursed as pain coursed up her arm.

"Hey. It's okay." Hudson came to stand beside her and rubbed her shoulder.

"No, it's not okay, Hudson. It's far from okay." What if they'd hit Gran? Sunny's shoulders went rigid. Blood pounded through her veins. She was done with turning the other cheek. She'd make the bastards who'd done this pay.

"Now, don't you be getting any ideas in that head of yours or go looking for trouble," her grandmother said

Sunny turned and saw her grandmother standing in the short hallway with the shotgun at her hip. Gran's graying hair was all mussed up, and her skin was almost parchment white. All the fight left Sunny. She went over and wrapped her arms around her grandmother. The last thing she'd wanted to do was bring trouble to Gran's door, and now the woman was walking around with a shotgun.

Her grandmother hugged her tightly and then let her go. "Don't be worrying about me. I'm fine, and we'll have the window fixed in a jiffy. I've already called John Morris. He'll be over shortly to board it up, and he'll order a new window for us. It'll be good as new in a couple of days."

Sirens wailed in the distance but grew ever closer. *Great. More attention.* All she wanted to do was run. Run far. Run fast. Run so her grandmother would be safe. Run so she wouldn't be sent to prison for a murder she didn't commit. Run so she wouldn't have to be next to Hudson, whose closeness still made her belly do flips like she was on a ride at the fair.

70

Sunny hurried to the kitchen. She grabbed a rag and the broom with the dustpan, then climbed the stairs to clean up the mess she'd made. Anything was better than standing around doing nothing. She'd never felt so helpless in her whole life. Her shoulders slumped, her hand ached, and she must have fallen on her right knee because it was throbbing as well.

Hudson murmured something to her grandmother and went out the front door. The sirens stopped. Colin must have arrived. That would be three times she'd seen him in one day. She came down the stairs, dustpan full of broken china in hand. "I'm sorry, Gran. I'm so sorry."

Her grandmother's eyes filled with tears, but she took a deep breath and blinked them back. "There's not a thing for you to be sorry about," she said as she grabbed Sunny's arm and squeezed. "None of this is your fault. Do you hear me? None of it. Colin will get to the bottom of it. We'll have to keep going 'til then."

Sunny gave her grandmother a sad smile and then nodded. She didn't trust herself to speak. Instead, she stepped past her grandmother into the kitchen and threw the china in the garbage. And even though she wanted a shot of whiskey, she put on the kettle for more tea.

"Ms. Clara. Sorry 'bout what happened." Colin's voice floated down the hallway.

"Thank you kindly, Colin. Please find the person

or persons who did this. I would like them to pay for the damage."

"I'll do my best, ma'am."

Sunny made the tea and then walked down the hallway. She stood in the doorway to the parlor. Colin was standing between the coffee table and the TV. She nodded to him, and he nodded back. Hudson came to stand beside her, and his closeness warmed her arm. She hadn't realized until just that second how cold it was getting in the house. When she shivered, Hudson moved closer.

"Can you tell me what happened?" Colin asked.

Sunny cleared her throat. Truthfully, it was a little hard to concentrate standing this close to Hudson. The heat from his body, mixed with his scent, was a heady combination. He'd always been attractive, but now he was an adult—a man—and he was completely distracting.

"Sunny?"

"Uh, sorry, Colin. Right. I had just finished cleaning up the kitchen after dinner. I was going up the stairs with a mug of tea in my hand when the crash happened."

"Did you see anyone or hear anything before that?"

"No. Nothing."

"Were the lights on in the front of the house?" Colin asked.

"Ah, no. Why?"

Colin shrugged. "They might have thought the house was empty. It indicates the perp was probably just trying to scare you."

"Well, they succeeded." Sunny rubbed her arms.

Colin nodded. "You said John Morris is on the way?"

"Yes," Clara confirmed.

"He'll board it up. That's about all we can do tonight. I'll take the rock with me, but I doubt there'll be any prints on it. I'll ask around and see if anyone knows anything."

Sunny frowned. "I can read between the lines. You're saying it's unlikely you're gonna find out who did this."

"Sunny, you and Ms. Clara live out here on your own. Your nearest neighbor is a quarter mile away. There's not much of a chance anyone saw anything. Do you have security cameras?"

Sunny shook her head.

"Not yet, but they will. I'll install some tomorrow," Hudson said.

Sunny shot him a look. Where did he get off, making decisions for her and her grandmother? It wouldn't be cheap, and there were plenty of more important things that needed fixing around here. Not to mention the God-awful amount of money she was going to need for the murder trial.

She glanced at her grandmother. Any urge she had to fight with Hudson died. The old woman still looked ashen. Clara might have a mighty spirit, but her body was starting to fail her. "Gran, why don't you go sit and have a cup of tea in the kitchen? The blood pressure cuff is in there as well. Check it and let me know if you need another pill. I can take care of all this."

Her grandmother opened her mouth, presumably to argue, but then changed her mind and nodded.

"Ms. Clara, can I have the shotgun, please?" Colin asked.

"No," Gran said and then turned and walked back to the kitchen.

Colin looked surprised. He hadn't expected her to give it up, had he? Sunny clapped a hand over her mouth to stifle a giggle. She tried to pass it off as a cough and wound up sounding like some sort of wounded animal. Hudson started rubbing her back, but the sensation of his hand rubbing her flesh, even if it was to calm a non-existent cough, was too alluring. She stepped away and leaned against the stairwell.

Colin glanced at her hand, still wrapped in a towel. "And you didn't see or hear anything?"

"Just the window breaking."

Colin nodded. "Could have taken off on foot or had a vehicle parked down the road. I'll try and get someone over here in the morning to look for footprints or tire tracks." He was quiet for a moment, as if stewing on something, then he sighed. "I gotta be honest with you, Sunny, with things...the way they are, I'm not sure the chief is going to let me spend time or resources on this."

Sunny stood straight up, her hands on her hips. "Because he thinks I killed Wayne? That's not fair, Colin! My grandmother and I deserve to be treated like everyone else. What about innocent until proven guilty?"

Colin grimaced and raised his hands as if to placate her. "I know, Sunny, and I agree, but I'm telling you like it is. I'm sorry as hell about it."

His honesty made some of the fight leak out of her, and Sunny dropped her hands from her hips and leaned back against the stairwell.

Colin used a glove to pick up the rock and put it in a plastic evidence bag he'd pulled out of his pocket. "Is there anywhere else you could go, maybe?" he asked as he walked out of the parlor and stood inside the doorway. "Until things cool off a bit? I'm sure I can convince the chief that it's better for you to leave town for a while. He can talk Judge Goldsmith into anything. Those two are thick as thieves."

"No, Colin. There's nowhere to go. This mess would follow me." Sunny hated herself a little for how much she *wanted* to go. It would be amazing to run back to L.A. and forget Canyon Springs existed, but her grandmother would never go with her. Gran's whole life was here.

"I have no choice but to face up to it and try to

prove my innocence." Her shoulders drooped even more. It shouldn't be up to her to prove her innocence, they should have to prove her guilt. But, she was beginning to believe she wasn't going to get a fair shake in Canyon Springs and proving her innocence was damn hard when no one in town would speak to her.

Colin opened his mouth and then closed it again. He gave a short nod. "I'll get this back to the station and write it up. With any luck, I can get out here tomorrow and poke around a bit. Maybe something will turn up."

"Thank you." Sunny tried to smile, but it didn't work.

"I appreciate it, Colin," Hudson said.

"Say goodnight to your grandmother for me," Colin said, "and please remind her to be careful with that shotgun. I know she knows what she's doing. My wife says she sees Clara down at the shooting range occasionally, but I don't want anyone to get hurt."

"I'll remind her, Colin. And thanks for coming out."

Colin nodded and gave a small wave as he left and closed the door behind him.

Hudson turned and leaned on the doorjamb across from Sunny. "It's not a bad idea, you know."

Their gazes locked, and electricity danced across her skin. "I'm not running."

"I don't mean leaving town. I mean finding

another place to stay. It's gonna be cold in here until John shows up to cover the windows. Even then, it won't be super warm. It's fall in the mountains. The temperature drops with the sun. Halloween is just around the corner." Hudson shifted and stuck his hands in the pockets of his well-worn jeans. "I'm also worried someone could come back. Everyone in town knows where you live."

"They wouldn't do that, at least not tonight."

Hudson raised an eyebrow. "Are you sure about that? What if the real murderer is out to do you harm? Do you want to take that risk?" He flicked his gaze toward the kitchen and then back at Sunny.

Damn it. He was right. No matter how unlikely it was, there was still a slim chance someone might come back to attack them. As to the real murderer, why would they want to hurt her? She was the perfect patsy.

No. She couldn't risk it. Gran's "spells," as she called them, were getting worse, and stress wouldn't help. But did she trust Hudson? She cocked her head and narrowed her eyes. "What are you suggesting?"

Hudson's voice got husky. "Why don't you and Clara come out to my mom's place with me?"

She started shaking her head before he even finished the sentence. "No. No way."

"Hear me out." Hudson demanded. He swallowed and started again in a softer voice. "I have a friend staying with me. He's one of the guys from my old unit in the SEALs, and now he's been doing personal security with me overseas. That means there'd be two of us to keep you and your grandmother safe. We have plenty of room at the house, and there'd be more people around in general."

"He's right," Gran said as she walked back into the hallway. "About some things anyway. You'll be safer at his place. It's bigger, but with all the ranch hands around and the people he's got working to fix it all up, anyone would be hard pressed to do something without the world seeing it. And you always liked the ranch."

"Ms. Clara, I think you should come, too. You can't stay here on your own."

Sunny frowned. "She's not planning on staying here. She's going into town to stay with Nancy and June, right?"

Gran nodded.

"They've been having sleepovers since June's husband passed away a few years ago and Nancy moved in. The girls wouldn't want Gran to stay anywhere else."

Hudson smiled. "I guess that would work. They're right in town, and anyone who's been in town for a hot minute will know better than to mess with Nancy and June."

Gran nodded. "Jeb's on the way to get me. He'll be here shortly. I'm going to pack my bag." She gave Sunny a pointed look. "I suggest you do the same, missy. You will be staying with Hudson for the foreseeable future."

Sunny ground her teeth. This was the last thing she wanted. The absolute. Last. Thing. But she wasn't going to argue. Her grandmother was exhausted and needed to be surrounded by friends. She needed to be safe and Sunny couldn't stay with Nancy and June, putting all three of them at greater risk. There was no way she'd leave if Sunny refused to do the same. Which meant she had no choice. Sunny told herself it didn't matter—she would stay strong no matter what people (literally) threw at her. Burgers or rocks be damned. She could survive being close to Hudson Riggs, too.

So why did that sound like a lie?

CHAPTER 8

HUDSON DIDN'T KNOW if this was a great idea or the dumbest he'd ever had. Having Sunny in the truck next to him was bad enough, but having her at the house for the foreseeable future would be absolute torture.

The sound of the glass shattering had been like taking one to his bulletproof vest. All the air had rushed out of his lungs, and he hadn't breathed again until he saw Sunny standing there in the hallway. She'd been so scared; it'd taken all the restraint he possessed not to take her in his arms and crush her to his chest.

He ran a hand through his hair. Maybe he should call Hank and tell him to find someone else for this job because he was too damn close to Sunny to be able to think clearly. He'd pay for the service.

Who was he kidding? No way in hell would he let

anyone else get near Sunny. He would protect her even if it killed him or gave him the worst case of blue balls he'd ever had. It was a toss up which would happen first.

They pulled into the long driveway of his mom's ranch. It was a dark night, but he'd had Rhys turn on the lights that lit up the fence line. It made it seem more homey and cheerful somehow. Or at least he hoped it did. Sunny's day had been bad enough—he didn't want her forced exile to the ranch to be miserable, too.

Her phone buzzed, and she looked down in her lap. "Jed just dropped Gran off at June and Nancy's."

"Good. Colin offered to have one of the night-shift guys to drive by their place every so often."

Sunny's shoulders dropped a tiny bit. "Thanks. I appreciate it."

He rolled to a stop beside the house. "I think Clara will be fine there. No one wants to hurt her or cause her problems. She's well-respected in town."

"Unlike me." Her shoulders went back up.

Shit. "That's not what I meant."

"Forget it. I understand." Her icy tone indicated she didn't.

"Sunny," he started, but she'd already opened the door and hopped out of the truck.

Huck ran over and gave him a quick nosing before racing around the truck to greet Sunny. "That's—"

"Huck. Yeah, we're old friends, aren't we?" Sunny said as she scratched him behind the ears. "How's my handsome boy? Hmmm?" She petted Huck some more and then finally straightened up.

Hudson frowned. "How do you know Huck?"

Sunny turned and grabbed her bag out of the back of the truck. "I've come up here a couple of times to meet with your mom. She's on every committee in town, and when we started to offer catering at the diner, she helped me figure out what options would be the most desirable."

"Oh. I had no idea."

"Why would you? You weren't here." Sunny started walking toward the front porch.

Ouch. That one hit home. Hudson rubbed his chest. He should've kept in touch. He shook his head. He shouldn't have left in the first place, at least not without talking to Sunny face to face first. The note he left didn't say much other than he had to go. Should've, could've, would've... Hindsight was twenty-twenty.

The door opened, and Rhys came out and moved over to the railing.

"Sunny, this is a good friend of mine, Rhys Beckett."

Sunny reached the top step and started to offer her hand, but she lowered it when she saw the towel still wrapped around it. "It's nice to meet you."

Rhys smiled at her, not fazed by the bloody towel. "Nice to meet you, too. I've heard a lot about you."

"Oh, really?" Sunny turned and glared at Hudson. At least he thought it was a glare. It was hard to tell with the light behind her. "Well, I hope at least some of it was good."

"All of it," Rhys said, "and it didn't remotely do you justice. Can I help you with your bag?"

But before he could reach for it, Hudson hurtled up the stairs. He took the bag and put his hand on the small of Sunny's back to usher her inside. She stiffened under his touch, and Hudson swore a blue streak in his head.

Rhys turned his head away as he opened the door for them, but Hudson still saw his smirk. *Asshole.* He couldn't help it if the mere hint of flirtation between Rhys, who was known for his lady-slaying ways, and Sunny had made the blood thunder in his ears.

They all piled into the foyer and stopped. It was essentially the same layout as Clara's place, but much larger.

Hudson guided Sunny into the huge great room. "Why don't you have a seat in front of the fire? I'll grab the first-aid kit and we'll fix up your hand." He pointed to a large worn leather chair and ottoman by the fireplace.

It had been his father's favorite spot growing up, and now it was his mother's. She always sat there during their video chats. The gas fireplace had been turned on, something he'd asked Rhys to do over the phone.

"That's okay," Sunny said. The response was so quick to fly off her tongue he had a sense she was used to telling people she was okay even when she wasn't. She glanced down at the bloody towel. "You know, I guess maybe you're right."

Hudson smiled. One less argument they had to have. "Let me put your stuff up in your room. I'll be right back." He took off and went up the stairs two at a time. He didn't want to leave Sunny alone for long, not after the day she'd had. And, okay, Rhys was down there, but he didn't want to leave her alone with him so much either.

He opened the door to the flower room, as his mother called it. The whole thing was done in flower prints. The curtains, the wallpaper, and even the bedspread. It was way too much, to Hudson's way of thinking, but his mom loved it…and he thought maybe Sunny would, too.

He dropped her bag on the bed, checked the adjoining bathroom to make sure there were enough towels, and then grabbed the first-aid kit from under the sink and a bottle of aspirin from the cabinet. He headed back downstairs.

Rhys had settled on the old brown leather couch across from Sunny's chair, and when Hudson entered the room, he was asking her about the spa.

"So it's in trouble?" Rhys asked. "The spa? I have

an appointment with some new doctor there tomorrow. Seems odd to see a doctor at a spa."

That was news to Hudson. He was glad his friend had a change of heart about seeing the specialist. About damn time he started taking care of himself. He didn't tell Rhys, but he was slightly worried. His leg should have been better by now. It was the real reason he'd invited Rhys. Their boss Josh Baker had asked him to get Rhys back stateside and get him to see a specialist.

"It appears so. People say it's going under. I have to say it seems odd. The place is always packed, and celebrities and wealthy people have been going there for years. It's a spa and medical center all mixed together. More of a wellness center than just one or the other."

She took a sip from the glass in her hand. "Canyon Springs might be a small town, but there's a private airport, and we're close to Missoula, so celebs and the like can come here without everyone knowing about it and still have access to all the amenities they want. I can't think why it would fail."

Hudson frowned slightly as he approached them. The glass was filled with amber liquid and some ice cubes. Bourbon if he had to guess. Rhys had one, too, but that was no surprise—it was his drink of choice. He'd never known Sunny to drink, but then again, he'd left when they were still underage. Just another thing that had changed.

"Any idea who threw the rock through the window?" Rhys asked

Sunny shook her head. "No. I have no idea who's doing any of the stuff that keeps happening. Well, other than jerk who threw his food at me earlier."

Hudson held up the first-aid kit as he plunked down on the ottoman in front of Sunny. "That was his daughter Marla with him at the diner today, wasn't it? She was a few years ahead of us, right? Where's she stand on all of this?"

She shrugged. "Two years ahead of you and three ahead of me. It's like I told you—Byron thought Wayne was going to help Marla's son. She had Jackson about a year after finishing high school." She made a face. "She did date Wayne briefly at some point, but I think it was when Wayne and I were in tenth grade and it was just before she got pregnant. Wayne always looked much older. Anyway, he wasn't the father, and she never seemed too hung up on him."

Rhys rattled the ice cubes in his glass. "Sounds like this Wayne guy got around."

Sunny grimaced. "You could say that. He dated most of my senior class. Other than Marla and me, there was Tina, who currently runs the nail salon on Main Street, and Jenny, who owns the Green Bean Cafe. It's rumored he also dated several cheerleaders, including Kendra, Colin's wife."

Hudson blinked. "Kendra Hollister? She married Colin Edwards?"

"Who's Kendra Hollister, and why is it such a surprise she'd marry some guy named Colin Edwards?" Rhys asked then he drained his glass.

"Kendra Hollister was the head cheerleader," Sunny said. "She was super smart and beautiful. She desperately wanted out after graduation. Her family didn't have much money, and I remember she was trying for a scholarship so she could go to college." She took a sip of her drink. "We all wanted out back then. Anything to get away from this small town."

Hudson's guilt ratcheted up a notch. If he had stayed, they would have at least been here together that last year. Instead, he'd left and joined the Navy while Sunny was back here finishing school.

"Anyway," Sunny said, "Colin was the polar opposite. Smart but not brilliant and a real homebody. He was kind of scrawny in high school. A shy kid. But he's a cop now. He was the one who…arrested me."

"Sunny," Rhys said in a quiet voice, "do you have any idea who killed Wayne?"

Hudson shot Rhys a look. Although he'd given Rhys a rundown of the situation earlier, he'd warned him not to question Sunny too pointedly. He didn't want to scare her off. Nor did he want to pressure her, at least not tonight. But, as usual, Rhys ignored him and did his own thing.

"Hudson told me your overview of what happened that night when he called earlier. Can you remember anything that might help us find the real killer?"

Sunny scrunched up her face and shook her head. "I've been racking my brain, but I honestly have no clue. Wayne wasn't...the nicest guy back in high school and, honestly speaking, he didn't change. I think he was BSing the town about everything he claimed he was going to do here. Wayne would only do it if it helped Wayne."

She shrugged. "I think some people were starting to understand that. He had some sort of argument with Jenny the day I saw him at the Green Bean. I heard Jenny say something to the effect of, 'If you do that, it will ruin me!' Wayne smiled, grabbed his coffee, and sat down at my table."

Sunny took another sip of her drink. "I've been asking around, you know, trying to figure out who really killed Wayne. Kendra dropped by the diner one day, and I asked her if she had any ideas, but she didn't. I spoke with Tina but didn't get anywhere. She shut me down pretty quick, but then I spoke with June and Nancy. They said Tina's business partner, Mazie, had a run-in with Wayne, too. I even over-heard Mazie saying something about it at the nail salon, but then...well, I had to leave."

Hudson's chest felt like it was in a vise. The way everyone had up and turned on Sunny was one of the things he'd always hated so much about this town.

Sometimes there was a mob mentality—people would be with you one day and your worst enemy the next. He wanted to reach out and hold Sunny, but he knew she'd push him away.

"So, you think Wayne was making some enemies in town?" Rhys pressed.

Sunny nodded. "He made a lot of promises, but I didn't hear about a lot of follow through. Then again, I avoided him as much as I could, so I don't know."

Hudson shot Rhys another look and gave his head a slight shake. She needed to rest. They could ask her more questions later. "Now let's see that hand."

She took a sip of her drink, as if to bolster herself, and offered her wounded hand to Hudson.

Hudson unwrapped the towel slowly and tried to be gentle, but he saw her bite her lip. He tried not to stare. He remembered those lips. Soft, full, kissable.

He looked back down as he peeled off the last bit of cloth. He dropped the towel next to him and shifted her arm so it rested on his thigh, the wound closer to the light. Heat radiated off her arm, penetrating his jeans making him incredibly aware of her, and it was wrong to feel that way about her now with her injured hand splayed in front of him, and yet he did.

Reminding himself to focus—he was here to help her, not to kiss her—he pulled out the alcohol wipes and opened a couple. "This is going to sting," he said as he glanced up at her. He thought he saw an answering glimmer of desire in her eyes, but she blinked and turned away.

He touched the wipe to her hand, and she pulled back. He held firm. "Sorry, I need to make sure this is clean and there's no glass left in it." He didn't dare look up because, if she was biting her lip again, he was going to end up pulling her into his lap and kissing her until neither of them could breathe.

Maybe he was giving off that kind of vibe because Rhys stood from the couch. "I'm gonna head up to my room. Hud, do you need me to keep watch or anything?"

Hudson kept his head down and continued to clean Sunny's wound. "No. The cameras are up and running. I'll get an alert on my phone if anything triggers one of them. See you in the morning."

"'Night, Hud. 'Night, Sunny."

"Goodnight, Rhys. It was nice to meet you."

Was it his imagination or was her voice a bit breathy? He looked up again. Their eyes locked. His heart gave a thump in his chest. His hands tingled with the desire to touch her. He wanted to feel her skin underneath his fingers—soft and smooth, familiar and yet not. Electricity ran through his veins. This was no high school lust. This was full-on adult desire that had him wanting Sunny so badly he was in physical pain.

"I—you— That is..." Sunny stopped and licked her lips.

He followed the movement. It did nothing to help his current predicament. He shifted to ease his discomfort, pressed on the bandage, and cleared his throat. "Um, your hand looks fine. The cut isn't deep enough for stitches, but try and go easy on it for the next couple of days."

She nodded.

He let go of her hand and stood. It was still painful to walk, but he needed to get some distance between them. He walked over to the bar and got a beer out of the bar fridge. He wanted something stronger, but he needed to be alert in case anything else did happen tonight. Her scent seemed to follow him to the other side of the room, which shouldn't be any surprise—it had followed him across oceans.

He walked back over and lowered himself onto the couch where Rhys had been. "Do you want any pain meds for your hand?

"No," she said. For a moment, neither of them spoke, then she said his name, her voice still the slightest bit breathy. "You said Vince hired you to watch over me, but you didn't tell me how that happened. Did he call you up and ask? I didn't think you two knew each other. He didn't come to town until after you left. He's from Missoula."

Hudson had been dreading this moment. He wanted so much to tell her the truth, that he was here to protect her, not because he was getting paid but because he wanted to keep her safe. But Sunny would flip out if he told her. She would refuse his help, and he just couldn't take that risk.

He chose his words carefully. "A guy named Hank Patterson runs a personal security company out of Eagle Rock. I knew him when I was starting out in the military. He offered help to Vince if he needed any, and Vince mentioned your case. Anyway, I was getting a little bored. Mom has completely turned the ranch around since my dad just about ran it into the ground. Now it's running like clockwork, and it needs very little daily help from me. So I offered to take the job."

"Well"—she frowned—"I'm not sure how I'm going to pay for all this, but I promise I'll figure it out somehow."

"Don't worry about it now. We can deal with all that later."

Sunny covered her yawn with the back of her hand.

"It's been a long day," Hudson said, hoping he could distract Sunny so she'd drop the matter. "Why don't you head on up to bed? I'm going to take a quick look around before I lock things down."

"I *am* exhausted actually," she said with a tight smile. "I haven't been sleeping well." She started out of her chair and winced when she put pressure on her hand.

"I know you're not much on taking pills. Me

either, but I think an aspirin for your hand wouldn't hurt. Are you sure you don't want one?"

She started to shake her head but stopped. "You know what? You're right. I could use a good night's sleep, and my hand's throbbing."

Hudson gave a curt nod and hopped up off the couch. He grabbed the bottle of aspirin from the coffee table and popped the top, then circled around to put a pill on her upturned palm. "Stay right here, and I'll get you a glass of water."

"No need," she said as she popped the aspirin in her mouth and followed it with the last swig of bourbon from her glass.

Hudson blinked. "Well, that's one way to do it." Sexy as hell, too. Her scent hit him again, making his blood pound through his veins. Being close to her was killing him.

Sunny grinned. "I'm in the flower room, right?"

"How'd you know?" His voice sounded husky to his own ears. He tried to clear his throat.

"Rhys doesn't look like the flower type."

Hudson let out a low laugh. "Very true."

"Hudson," she said in a low voice, "thanks for your help tonight with Gran and...everything. I—"

"No problem. I'm glad you're okay." He reached out and brushed a lock of hair behind her ear. The gesture seemed so natural, so ordinary, but it broke some silent barrier between them. The next second she was in his arms and he was kissing her. He had no idea who made the first move, nor did he care. It felt right in a way it never had with anyone else.

Sunny opened her mouth, and he deepened the kiss. He wrapped his arms around her back and pulled her close, marveling at how familiar yet totally different this felt. She still fit perfect in his embrace, but this wasn't the kiss of a high schooler fooling around in the car. Sunny was a strong, driven woman, and she knew her own mind.

She fisted his hair and pulled him closer still, the sensation shooting straight to his cock. The urgency in the kiss intensified, and he was becoming completely lost in her. He cupped her ass and moved her against his length. She let off a soft moan.

Her hands moved down his chest and then went under his sweater. He damn near lost it when her fingers touched his skin. He needed to feel her naked against him—a need so urgent it was driving every bit of sense out of his mind.

There was a sudden bang, and Sunny jumped out of his arms. She looked at him, eyes wide open and wild.

Hudson swore. "It was Rhys. He dropped something on the floor in the room above us."

Sunny nodded, then turned on her heel and disappeared up the stairs.

He blinked. One minute she was touching him, and the next she was gone. What the hell had happened? *Damn it, Rhys.* He ran his hands through his hair and took a deep breath.

What if it had been something else? Another rock through the window maybe, or worse. He'd been so caught up in Sunny, he wouldn't have cared if the house had burned down around them. This was bad. He was supposed to be protecting her, but all he wanted to do was touch her. Taste her. Make her climax again and again.

And...this wasn't helping.

He squared his shoulders and grabbed the first-aid kit off the ottoman. He needed to do better. He had to keep her safe, even from *himself.* Because at the moment, they were in danger of ending up right back where they'd started all those years ago. And he didn't mind at all.

CHAPTER 9

Sunny woke up late. She got up quickly but pampered herself with a long, hot shower. She dressed in jeans and a black V-neck cashmere sweater she'd gotten on sale in her L.A. days. It wasn't that she wanted to look good for Hudson or anything —it was just a bit chilly was all.

Right.

It had taken her ages to calm down after that kiss. Heat blossomed in her cheeks just thinking about it…and it was going to start somewhere else again if she didn't stop dwelling.

She still felt like an idiot flying up the stairs like that but, damn it, he'd left her with only a stupid note in high school. She'd been absolutely crushed. He shouldn't be able to sweep back into town and pick up right where they left off. At the very least, he should get down on his knees and apologize.

Maybe he can do something else while he's down there.

She gave herself a mental shake and squared her shoulders before heading downstairs. She could smell the bacon as soon as she hit the bottom step. That delicious aroma led her to the kitchen like the Pied Piper. "Something smells good."

Hudson looked over his shoulder and smiled at her. "Pancakes and bacon with a side of scrambled eggs. Be ready in five minutes."

Sunny walked over and poured herself a cup of coffee. Pancakes and bacon were two of her favorite breakfast foods, right up there with eggs, fries, and tzatziki sauce.

Her mouth watered as she went over and sat down at the kitchen table. She tried not to stare at Hudson, but he was wearing a blue sweater the exact color of his eyes and his jeans hugged his ass in a way that made her fingers itch to touch it.

"How are you feeling?" Hudson asked as he rationed out food onto various platters.

She cleared her throat. "Um, much better, thanks. My hand doesn't hurt too much. The sleep helped, not to mention a nice long, hot shower. The hot water tank at Gran's is tiny." She tore her gaze away from his ass long enough to take a sip of coffee.

Hudson chuckled. "Maybe I can add replacing the hot water tank to the list of tasks your grandmother is making for me." He brought the platters over and set them on the table. "Are you hungry?"

Sunny's stomach chose that moment to growl loudly. She rubbed it, heat crawling up her cheeks.

Hudson laughed. "I'll take that as a yes." He handed her a plate and sat down opposite her.

"Where is Rhys?" she asked as she started serving herself. She added pancakes and arranged a few slices of bacon around the edges.

Hudson placed a small bowl of berries next to her coffee mug. "He's gone to see that doctor at the The Wellness Retreat .

Sunny spread butter onto the top of each pancake she had stacked on her plate. "They offer all kinds of interesting medical innovations. Like I said, there's every reason for it to be successful. I hope someone buys it and turns it around if it really is going under." She reached for the maple syrup and poured some over her stack, then took her first bite and almost swooned from joy. They were fantastic.

She opened her eyes and realized Hudson was still watching her. "Pancakes are still a favorite of yours, I see."

She nodded and swallowed. "I rarely let myself enjoy them, but these are fantastic."

Hudson smiled. "Thanks. I learned to perfect them overseas. You'd be amazed at the things that bring you the most joy when you're away from home."

Sunny took another bite of pancakes and added a

piece of bacon. He was right. As much as she'd loved L.A., she'd missed the way the leaves turned color in the autumn here, the cool breezes of fall and spring, and the sight of the mountains.

"I have to go into town today to do a couple of things. I know you're probably anxious and don't want to sit around out here but I think it's better if you keep a low profile." Hudson said and then took another bite of breakfast.

Disappointment pooled in Sunny's stomach. She hated to admit it, but she enjoyed being with Hudson. She wanted to spend more time with him. To get to know the man he'd become. And most of all, she wanted him to kiss her again.

Bad. Bad. Remember he left with just a short note. No face to face. Not acceptable.

Besides, he was only in town temporarily. Given enough time, he would leave again, and she couldn't let him take her heart with him this time. The problem was that it was still so easy to relax around him, and she needed that. She needed a refuge. She took a sip of coffee and then popped a couple of berries in her mouth. "I know you're right. It's safer if I stay here. I just hate sitting around."

"I know. Some things never change." He smiled. "Why don't you check out Mom's stash of books. I'm sure there's something you haven't read."

Sunny smiled slightly. "Sure." It was going to be a

long, dull day, but maybe that was better. All the excitement she was experiencing lately was of the negative variety, and she didn't need any more of that.

CHAPTER 10

HUDSON SCANNED Main Street out of habit and then backed into a parking spot. Always be ready for a quick getaway.

It all looked so normal. Who would've thought there was a killer on the loose? He got out of the truck and made his way into the pharmacy where he picked up a few things he needed.

He hit the sporting goods store where he placed an order for some stuff to be dropped off at the ranch, and then he went to the feed store.

"Hudson."

A voice call his name as he stood at the cash register. "Hey Colin."

"Got a minute?" the officer asked.

Hudson nodded. He finished paying and then met Colin out on the sidewalk. "What's up?"

"I wanted to check on Sunny. How is she?"

"Shaken up but fine. She's at the ranch so she's safe."

Colin nodded. "Good idea. I checked on Clara this morning, and she's all good as well. The chief is fighting me looking for the rock thrower. He says it's a waste of time."

Hudson shrugged. "I'm not surprised."

"Me either. Sorry about that."

Hudson nodded. "Thanks and thanks for checking in about Sunny."

Colin offered his hand. "Tell her to hang in there." The men shook, and Colin walked down the sidewalk toward the police station.

Hudson looked across the street at the Green Bean Roastery. He'd wanted to poke around and ask questions about Wayne's murder. He'd heard some rumors, and Sunny had mentioned Jenny the owner had a past with Wayne. Now seemed as good a time as any to follow up.

The Green Bean was crowded. Hudson joined the line and scanned the crowd. He recognized a few faces but no one who might know more about Wayne.

He reached the front of the line and stepped up to the counter. "Hi, Jenny."

"Hudson, how are you?"

"I'm good. Glad to be home for a bit."

Jenny nodded. "I'm sure. What can I get you?"

Hudson placed his order and then offered Jenny

his best heart-melting smile. "Do you have a minute to chat?"

Jenny blinked and smiled back. She tucked her hair behind her ears as a slight flush came to her cheeks. "Um…" She glanced at the long line and then at her other barista, then she nodded. "Give me a minute to make your drink, and I'll meet you at the back counter."

"Great." Hudson kept the smile going. It was his secret weapon. It always worked. Except on Sunny. She never fell for it. Not once. He walked over and leaned on the end counter.

Jenny came over a few minutes later, his drink in hand. "Here's the coffee."

"Thanks. How's business? Looks busy in here."

"Yes, it's going well. Knock on wood." Jenny glanced around and quickly knocked on the wooden cabinet door behind her. "What about you? The ranch keeping you busy?"

Hudson shrugged. "Not so much. I'm actually trying to help out Sunny. She's having a bit of a hard time of it lately."

Jenny nodded. "I know, and I think it's awful. I don't believe for a minute she killed Wayne, not that I'd blame her if she did."

"Why do you say that?" Hudson asked.

Jenny played with the stir sticks that had been left on the counter. "Ah, no reason I guess." She gave him a quick smile. "I should be getting back."

He was losing her. He leaned in closer to Jenny and dropped his voice. "Come on. You can tell me. I already know Wayne wasn't the good guy he pretended to be."

Jenny's eyes snapped up. "Exactly," she hissed. "Everyone in this town thought he was some sort of hero. He was a mean asshole. Now and then. We... I mean he—" Jenny licked her lips and then shrugged. "I might as well tell you. He threatened to open a cafe just down the street. At first, I thought he was saying it to get a rise out of me. He liked to do that, but then I saw him talking to Savanna Grant, the real estate agent with that listing. I asked him about it, and he laughed in my face." Jenny crossed her arms over her chest. "I'll tell you something. I'm not sorry he's dead. He was an awful person."

The vehemence in her voice made Hudson's inner alarm bells go off. She was not a happy woman. "Do you know anyone else he pissed off?"

"He'd been lying about shit all over town. A lot of people were gonna find out he wasn't who he said he was."

"Who specifically?" Hudson asked. He was pushing but he needed names.

Jenny straightened up. "I've got to get back. Look, I'm sorry Sunny's going through this. Tell her I was asking after her." She moved back down to work the cash register.

"Shit." Hudson mumbled. He'd pushed too hard.

Still, at least he knew a bit more. Wayne was making enemies. Now he had to find out who they were.

Twenty minutes later, Hudson pulled up to the ranch house. Huck ran out to greet him. Sunny waved. She was sitting on the porch.

Hudson's thoughts were cycling rapidly through his mind. After what he'd heard today, he was going to have to question Sunny again about Wayne Bradley. If he was going to clear her name, he needed to know the whole story.

Rhys came out and handed Sunny a mug as Hudson came up the steps. "Hey, what about me?"

"You want tea?" Rhys asked, eyebrows raised.

Hudson grunted. "You could have made coffee."

Rhys grinned. "I could've but I didn't."

"Thank you for the tea." Sunny smiled briefly at Rhys. "So you were saying about your family. How many sisters do you have?"

"Five."

Sunny coughed on her tea. "That's a lot of sisters," she rasped.

Rhys nodded. "Yes, it is. Now you know why I'm here and not back home in North Carolina."

HUDSON WENT INSIDE and hit the button on the coffee maker. It started its whirring and grinding. He sighed. How the hell was he supposed to broach the topic of Sunny's romantic history with Wayne? She clearly didn't want to discuss it. But when he took his coffee out to the porch, Rhys had already done the asking.

"I don't remember how it started," Sunny was saying. "He asked, I guess, and we just started dating. You know how it is in high school."

It was exactly what Hudson had wanted to ask her about, but somehow he didn't feel relieved. He'd hoped she would open up to him, not his friend. But he didn't interfere. As much as it rankled him, he would let Rhys ask the questions because Sunny seemed to be responding better to him. He ground his teeth as he leaned his ass against the porch railing in front of Sunny.

"How long did you date for?" Rhys's voice was gentle.

Sunny frowned. "I don't remember exactly. A couple of months maybe? It started at the end of the year, before Christmas. Wayne told me he'd liked me all through high school, but I was with Hudson, so he never had a chance to ask me out." She took a sip of her tea.

Rhys and Hudson exchanged a glance.

"Sunny," Hudson said softly, "I spoke to Jenny today. She said Wayne wasn't nice. It didn't sound like she was talking about him being a player. What did she mean?"

Sunny had been staring off into the mountains, but she turned and looked at Hudson. Some sort of inner struggle played out in her eyes. Finally, she shrugged and then snuggled into her wrap. "Wayne was considered to be a catch back then. You were gone, and there weren't that many guys in school that were going places. I think it sort of went to his head. I mean, he always had a temper but...it got worse that year."

Hudson's gut churned. He sensed something bad was coming, but it had already happened so he had no way of stopping it.

Sunny took a sip of tea. "We had gone to see a movie, and I wanted plain popcorn. I hate that chemical crap they call butter."

"I remember," Hudson said with a smile.

"Well, Wayne bought a big bucket for us to share, but he put the fake butter on it. I said I didn't want any. He said it would taste fine, but I said I wasn't eating it." She paused and glanced down.

Hudson's heartbeat ticked up in his chest.

She looked up at him. "That was the first time I ever saw someone get mad. Like really mad. He lost it. He started yelling at me, but realized he was making a scene so he grabbed my arm and pulled me out the side door to the alley."

Hudson's knuckles were now white against his mug.

"He flew into a rage and pushed me up against the wall. He called me a cock-tease and a stupid bitch." Sunny hesitated. She gripped the arm of the chair with her free hand as she continued. "I turned away from him and started to run down the alley. He caught up to me and grabbed me by the arm. He turned me around and backhanded me so hard I went flying and landed on my back. I must have banged my head because I remember seeing stars."

Hudson couldn't breathe. He was having trouble hearing her words over the sound of his heart hammering in his chest.

"Anyway, old Mr. Ruggle happened to come into the alley. He demanded to know what was going on. I got up and ran back through the side door into the movie theatre. I hid in the bathroom and called Gran to come get me."

Hudson's gaze narrowed. He wanted to be calm, supportive, but his blood was roaring through his veins.

"Wayne came by to apologize the next day, but Gran had her shotgun and told him if he ever came near me again, she'd shoot him. He left, but on Monday, he told the world he'd dumped me because I was a cock-tease and not worth the effort."

Hudson tried to focus. He needed to pull himself together for Sunny's sake, but he couldn't stop thinking that Wayne Bradley was a lucky fucker after all since he didn't have to come face to face with Hudson.

"Hudson? Are you okay?" Sunny asked. "You don't look so good."

Her question, her honest concern for him, almost broke him. All the fight left his body, and guilt rushed in to take its place. He opened his mouth to speak but no sound came out. He cleared his throat and tried again. "Sunny, I'm so sorry you had to go through that, honey. If there was a way I could change it, I would."

She gave him a soft smile. "It was long ago, and it didn't take me long to get over it. Wayne dated plenty of other girls before we graduated. I tried to warn them. Jenny, Tina, even Kendra, but none of them believed me until he did it to them. I think by the end of that year, there was no one left in town for him to date."

"Does your lawyer know about this?" Rhys asked.

Sunny nodded.

Rhys went on, "Does that hurt or help your case?"

"Shit," Hudson said. He was still trying to gather his thoughts, but Rhys had already moved on to interpreting what this would mean for them.

"You're thinking it gives me motive. Vince and I talked about it. He thinks the prosecution is going to say that Wayne tried to attack me again that night, and I killed him."

"Wouldn't that be self-defense?" Rhys asked.

"Someone came up behind Wayne and choked the life out of him with my scarf. There's no way it was self-defense."

"Which means their theory doesn't work," Hudson said.

"That's what Vince says."

"Wayne put up a bit of a fight, and I didn't have any wounds. Still, he was zoned out on pain meds mixed with alcohol, so no one's sure how much of a defense he would have put up."

"Do you remember anything else from that night that could help you?" Hudson asked.

Sunny shook her head. "No. And I've been trying, believe me."

Her sad, broken look raked Hudson's heart. He needed to figure out a way to help her, to make this all go away, but he also wanted to give her some happiness. Some peace of mind. Or at least a few moments of distraction. The horses in the paddock whinnied, and an idea took hold of him. Something to make her feel better. Something to bring a little color back to her cheeks.

"Sunny, do you want to go for a ride? I need to exercise Dancer. He's not getting his usual runs with Mom gone."

She bit her lip. "I haven't been on a horse in a long time."

"It's like riding a bike. C'mon, it'll be fun. I'll throw together some food, and we can have a late lunch up on the hills. I think we both could use the break." Hudson glanced at Rhys.

He raised his hands. "I'm not riding with this leg.

Plus, my ass hasn't been in a saddle in a long time. I don't think I could take it."

She looked out at the fields and nodded slowly. "A ride would be nice."

"Great. I think there's some extra riding pants in the closet in your room, or you can go in your jeans. I'll get Gus to saddle up Dancer and Peanut." He hurried down the stairs, already wondering why he'd suggested something that would put them alone together. He was desperate to make her feel better.

No doubt about it, spending time with Sunny was playing hell with his equilibrium.

CHAPTER 11

SUNNY DREW in a lungful of mountain air and smiled. She'd forgotten how much she enjoyed riding. Peanut turned out to be a sorrel-colored mare that was incredibly gentle and sweet-tempered. Sunny couldn't have asked for a better horse.

The trail was a nice surprise, too. It wound up through the trees in such a slow, gradual zigzag that Sunny hadn't realized how high they were getting until there was a break in the tree line. It was such a beautiful day, and the fall leaves were an explosion of color all around them. Huck ran ahead on the trail and then came back again. His tongue was hanging out, and he was smiling in the way only dogs could.

Here, on this horse, in this place, with *Hudson*, she actually believed good things could happen again. Hudson. Her knees had almost given out when she walked into the barn.

He was standing there, brushing off Dancer. His blue sweater pulled tight across this arms and shoulders with every stroke. And those jeans, dear God, they hugged his ass in a way that made her hot all over.

She'd just about had herself under control when he turned around. The cowboy hat in combination with his sparkling deep blue eyes, he was the cover of a Cowboy romance novel come to life. She literally couldn't breathe. She'd had to lean against the stable door. Even now just thinking about it, she was getting all fired up. Good thing Hudson was *behind* her on Dancer. Last thing she needed was for him to turn around and see her in a state.

He called to her, and she looked over her shoulder. "I was thinking we could stop up ahead. There's a flat little meadow by the stream before the hillside falls away. It has a good view of the ranch.

"Sure. Um, that sounds great." Sunny's stomach growled since stopping would mean *food*, but thankfully Hudson was too far away to hear it. They pulled off the little trail and dismounted. Once Peanut's lead was securely tied to a tree, Sunny tried to help Hudson with the picnic stuff, but he waved her off.

While he was fighting with Huck, who had grabbed the blanket and wanted a game of tug-of-war, she wandered over to the stream and took in the view. It was spectacular. The whole ranch was laid out below them, and more rolling hills and mountains rose up beyond it. The meadow itself was beautiful. The grass was fading, but there were a few wildflowers left. It was a reminder that fall had well and truly arrived.

Hudson finally laid out the blanket and the picnic basket, and Sunny left the view to join him. "So, what did you bring us to eat?"

"You're starving, aren't you?" Hudson laughed. "I thought you might be once you got up here. Let's see." He brought out some roast beef sandwiches and cheese and crackers. He also had berries and cookies for dessert. Huck was lounging on the grass a few feet away, happily munching on a bone.

"Yum. You did a great job," she said as she reached for a sandwich.

Hudson handed her a plate and a bottle of water. "I thought about bringing some adult beverages, but if you haven't been on a horse for a while, drinking might not be the best idea."

Sunny laughed. "You're right. Peanut is a wonderful horse, but it's probably best if I don't drink and ride."

They ate in a companionable silence, Sunny gazing down at the valley as light played across the scene. It almost felt like her problems would go away if she stayed up here. She sighed. If only it could be that easy. Reality always came knocking. Soon there would be snow, and it would be brutally cold.

"Penny for 'em," Hudson said as he took off his

cowboy hat and stretched out on the blanket. He put the hat over his face.

Sunny quickly started clearing up everything and putting the remains of the picnic back in the basket. She was not about to tell him she was lusting after his body when he stretched out like that.

She cleared her throat. "Running never helps."

Hudson lifted his hat and looked at her, eyebrow cocked, his eyes serious. "Are you telling me this for a reason?"

"What?" Sunny blinked. *Shit.* He thought she meant him. "No. You asked what I was thinking, and that's it. Running never helps. Gran taught me that. Facing things means you deal with them." She put the last of the lunch back in the basket. "I was daydreaming how nice it would be to stay up here away from it all, but then the cold and the snow would come, and it wouldn't be fun anymore."

"Except cold and snow can be fun it you know what to do with it." Hudson's voice had taken on a husky quality that had Sunny's skin tingling.

She took a sip of water. "Maybe," was all she said. She moved the basket to the grass so she could stretch out her legs in front of her. Hudson dropped the hat back over his eyes, which Sunny took as an invitation to drink him in again.

His chest was all muscle, and she loved the V of his wide shoulders to his narrow hips. His thighs were no joke either. The men in L.A. all had runner's legs. Long, thin muscles. Always reminded her of chicken legs. Hudson's thighs were well muscled the way a man's thighs should be. Her fingers itched to touch him.

"Like what you see?" his asked as his lips curved into a big smile.

Bastard. He knew she did. She bit her lip, heat blooming across her cheeks. She was so busted. "Maybe," she said again, her voice barely above a whisper. She wanted him. Right now. She knew all the reasons she should get back on the horse and head to the house—hell, he still hadn't apologized for the last time he'd up and left—but if she'd learned one thing from all this, it was that life was short.

"Screw it," she mumbled as she rolled over onto her side next to Hudson. She moved her leg across the top of his thighs as she lifted his hat and threw it on the grass.

His eyes locked with hers, the lust in them undeniable. Her heart hammered in her chest and heat raced along her skin. She slid her hand up under his sweater and ran it across his chest. The muscles contracted under her fingers.

She'd longed for this from the moment she'd seen him at the diner. She wanted to feel him again. To touch him. To *taste* him. It wouldn't be the same as when they were kids. It would be so much better.

Huck let out a loud, piercing bark. In a flash, Hudson rolled her on her back and covered her with his body. She had a dizzying sense of excitement, but then the ground next to her head exploded, clods of grass and dirt landing on them.

She heard the report of the rifle. The horses whinnied. Hudson kept them rolling until they hit the tree line. The tree bark exploded above her head. Her entire body froze including her vocal cords. She couldn't utter a sound.

"Sunny!" Hudson whispered. "I need you to focus. We're too exposed here. You need to crawl on your belly into the trees. Go back toward the horses. I'll be right behind you. Stay as low as you can."

She blinked. She heard the words, but she couldn't make her body obey. One moment they'd been about to...enjoy themselves, and now they were fighting for their lives.

"Sunny, now!" Hudson barked as wood exploded from the side of the tree next to them.

Sunny rolled onto her belly and started crawling. Her lungs were on fire. Her breath came in great heaving gasps. She moved as quickly as she could, but it took forever to reach Peanut. When she did reach the horses, she hesitated to get closer because Peanut and Dancer were both prancing back and forth in agitation.

Hudson crawled up beside her. "I'm gonna need you to get on Peanut and go down the trail as fast as you can. Whoever this is won't have a clear shot at you on the trail. Too many trees. Trust Peanut. She can handle herself. She'll head for home on her own. Rhys will meet you at the tree line to take you to the house. Go!"

Sunny nodded. "What are you going to do?"

"I'm gonna go find this fucker!" Hudson leaned in and kissed her hard on the mouth and then crawled away into the trees.

Fear nearly paralyzed her. He was going to get himself killed, or she would be killed.

"Hudson, wait!" she whispered as loud as she dared, but he was already gone. A quick scan of the area revealed nothing, but then again, Sunny hadn't the first clue what to look for. Where was Huck? She'd lost track of him after his first bark.

Her palms were slick with sweat. Her heartbeat hammered her ribcage. Maybe if she stayed here in the trees outside the meadow, Hudson would find her when he got back, and they could go down to the house together.

Then she heard her Gran's voice telling her not to be stupid. *The shooter knows where you are.* She had to move. To be strong.

Tears blurred her vision, but she took a deep breath and leapt to her feet. Working as quickly as she could, she untied Peanut and struggled to get in the saddle. It wasn't easy because the horse wouldn't stay still, but finally she mounted. She turned Peanut downhill and gave her a nudge. It was all the urging the horse needed to take off. Sunny held on as tightly as she could, terrified Peanut would fall or buck her off, but the little horse was as sure-footed as she was swift.

She forced Peanut to stop before the end of the trail. The little horse was out of breath and so was Sunny. Her hands shook as she waited for Rhys. It was all wide-open pasture from here with nowhere to hide.

She heard the sound of the engine before she saw the pickup come up over the rise. Rhys arrived with two other pickup trucks trailing behind him, one on either side. There were guys with rifles in the back of each truck. Rhys motioned for her to come to him. Sunny nodded, but as she swung her leg over Peanut's back, she knew her knees wouldn't hold her. She ended up crashing to the ground.

Rhys was out of the truck and beside her in a heartbeat. "Are you hurt?"

She shook her head. "J-j-just s-s-cared." Her teeth were chattering. "M-my k-knees," she mumbled, and Rhys nodded. He scooped her up in his arms. The men with the guns were all scanning the tree line, rifles ready. Rhys curled his shoulders over her as he sprinted back to the truck. He dumped her into the driver's side of the truck, and she quickly scrambled across the bench seat to make room for him. Huck followed her in.

"Where did you come from?" she asked him. He gave a quick bark.

"Get down," Rhys said as he spun the truck around and headed back toward the ranch at full speed. He slammed on the brakes and slid across the grass until the passenger side door was equal to the front steps. There were men on the front porch, all armed, all ready for battle, something that was both reassuring and terrifying. Rhys turned to her. "Open your door and run into the house. The guys will keep you safe. I'm going back to help Hudson."

Sunny had a million questions, but the look on Rhys's face made her heart stop. "Is he hurt?"

"Sunny, go!"

Sunny lit out of the truck like it was on fire. She was up the stairs and in the house in a fraction of a second. She tripped over the rug in the foyer and landed on the floor. Huck ran right in behind her. He licked her face and her hands, worry written across his little doggy face. For some reason, that was what broke her. Sunny burst into tears. She buried her face in Huck's fur and sobbed.

CHAPTER 12

HUDSON YANKED open the screen door and stomped into the house. He was beyond pissed that they'd missed the shooter, and no matter how many people told him Sunny was fine, he wouldn't believe it until he saw her with his own eyes. He strode into the great room looking for her.

Sunny was curled up in the big leather chair by the fireplace with Huck beside her. She was wearing sweatpants and an oversize sweater. One of his, if he wasn't mistaken. She looked up when he entered. Her face was pale, and it was obvious she'd been crying. Hudson's chest was tight. He wanted to snap the neck of the person who'd tried to hurt Sunny. To *kill* her. He crossed the room and dropped down beside her chair. "I am so sorry."

Her eyes filled with tears. It was as if someone had grabbed his stomach and twisted as hard as they could. He couldn't breathe. In all his time overseas, he'd never felt as helpless as he did right now. "Oh, God, Sunny, please don't cry." He stood up and pulled her out of the chair to her feet and then wrapped his arms around her as tightly as he could. Her body shook with her tears. He swore long and loud.

Finally, Sunny pushed a little against his chest. "Hudson, I can't breathe."

He smiled slightly as he relaxed his hold but didn't let go. He didn't think he'd ever be able to let go again. The idea that Sunny might disappear from his life was too much. He wasn't having it.

"Did you find the person who shot at us?" Sunny's voice was soft.

"No," Hudson ground out. "He got too much of a lead." There were tracks from some kind of dirt bike, but they faded out.

A shudder ran through Sunny's body, and Hudson tightened his hold again. Sunny fit perfectly against him. She always had. He wanted to pick up where they'd left off up on the mountain. They'd barely gotten started thanks to the shooter. Another reason to hate the person.

"Hudson"—Sunny pushed against his chest—"I want to sit." She wouldn't meet his gaze.

Hudson very reluctantly let her go and watched as she lowered into the chair next to Huck. He crashed down on the ottoman across from her. "Looks like someone raided my closet."

Sunny sneaked a glance at him and sniffed. "I'm sorry. I was just so cold."

Sorry? He was overjoyed she was wearing his sweater. He'd love to see her in one of his T-shirts. It would be long enough on her to skim the tops of her thighs. He'd love to see her out of it even more. But that train of thought wasn't helpful, and it would only lead to him undressing her right here, right now.

He cleared his throat. "You can keep it if you want. Navy blue suits you." He reached out and curled a lock of her hair around his finger. "It brings out the color of your hair."

She looked up, and their gazes locked. He wanted to say so many things—he ached with them. But "I'm sorry" didn't seem like it was enough, and "I want you so badly my balls hurt" probably wasn't the best choice either. He'd always sucked at finding words for his feelings. It was one of the many reasons he'd left with a quick note. What could he have said then? What could he say now?

Hudson cleared his throat. "The police chief came by. I spoke with him and told him what happened. He said we'd have to go down to the station sometime in the next few days to make a statement."

She nodded. "What else did he say?"

Hudson hesitated and then shrugged. "I wouldn't hold out too much hope there. He doesn't seem too keen on investigating. I think Colin told him about the other stuff that's been happening, and now he thinks it's part of that. His exact words were, 'Teenagers are stupid. This is just them giving Sunny a hard time.'"

Sunny's eyes narrowed. "He won't help then."

Hudson shook his head. He'd wanted to argue with the chief, but there didn't seem to be a point. It drove Hudson crazy, and he'd wanted to pop the guy one, but it wouldn't help matters.

Hudson grabbed Sunny's hands. He didn't want to bring it up, but he had to ask. "Sunny, can you think of any reason someone would shoot at you other than because of Wayne?"

She looked at him and blinked. "Seriously? What could I possibly have done to have someone shooting at me? They don't like the new menu at the diner?" She rolled her eyes.

Hudson sighed.

She pulled her hands from his and jumped up from the chair. "I don't know who killed Wayne, and I don't know who would want to kill me!" She turned and ran from the room. He heard her footsteps on the stairs.

"Ah, fuck!" he said as he turned and went after her. He took the stairs two at a time, but he hesitated when he reached her bedroom door. Maybe he should leave her alone. He was obviously no good at talking. But that was the coward's way out. And despite the way he'd left town all those years ago, he wasn't a coward. It was time for him to face up to Sunny's wrath…even if he'd sooner face a group of enemy soldiers in the hills of Afghanistan.

"Sunny?" He knocked softly. There was no response.

"Sunny?" He knocked harder. What if she was sobbing too hard to open the door? The thought made his gut roll. He hated it when women cried, and it was absolute torture when Sunny did.

Still, he raised his hand for another knock, but Sunny beat him to it. She opened the door, her face red and her eyes narrow. There was no mistaking that glare. "What?!"

Hudson blinked. "I—" She turned around and stormed to the other side of the room.

Hudson paused, then followed her in and shut the door behind him. "Sunny, I'm trying to find out what's going on."

She whirled and faced him. "And somehow this is all my fault, is that it?"

"What? No!" He crossed the room until he was standing directly in front of her.

"So what is it then?" she demanded, hands on hips.

She was so close. Her scent surrounded him. Heat radiated off her, hitting him straight in the groin in a sensual overload. He wanted her like he'd never wanted anyone in his life. And he couldn't pretend otherwise.

Pulling Sunny to him, he captured her mouth in a scorching kiss. Except this time, she didn't kiss him back. She froze under his touch, and he immediately pulled back. "Sunny, I'm sorry. I don't, I didn't—"

"Shut up, Hudson, and listen carefully because I'm only going to say this once. This is a bad idea. You and me. You're going to head out of town eventually, like you did last time, and unless I'm sent to prison, I'll still be here."

"You aren't going to—"

"Shut. Up." She glared at him. "You deserted me once, and the fact that I'm even speaking to you is a miracle you should be thankful for."

He *was* thankful. She would never know how much. "About that—"

"Hudson Riggs, if you don't shut your mouth, you won't get laid. Am I making myself clear?"

Hudson blinked. Laid? Then he nodded, afraid to open his mouth. Being with Sunny was all he could think about.

"Good." Sunny put her hands on her hips. "This is a bad idea. I'm scared and worn out. I'm also angry and hurt and desperate. Those are all terrible reasons to sleep with someone." She licked her lips, and Hudson couldn't help but follow her tongue's path with his eyes. "But that doesn't change the fact that I want you to hold me tonight. That I want to feel you next to me. Inside me. As much as you hurt me back then, I'm an adult now, and I'm just asking you for one night. Nothing beyond that." She held his gaze. "Do you agree?"

Hudson wanted her so badly he couldn't see straight. And although he knew one night would never be enough, he would take her on any terms he could get her. He nodded.

"Good." She put her hands on his chest and went up on her toes. She brushed her lips lightly against his, fingers digging into his sweater.

"Can I open my mouth now?" he growled.

"You'd better."

It was all he needed. He claimed her lips, his tongue plunging into her mouth, dancing with hers. Her sweet taste assaulted Hudson's senses and brought back memories charged with longing. He deepened the kiss and pulled her hips closer, desperate to feel every inch of her pressed against him.

When she wove a hand into his hair and whispered his name, a wave of fierce possession washed over him. He claimed her mouth again in a fiery kiss, as if she were his drug and he wanted to consume every bit of her. He was going to keep taking as long as he could. And he was going to give like he never had before.

If he only had one night with Sunny, it was going to be a night neither of them would ever forget.

CHAPTER 13

SUNNY LIFTED Hudson's sweater and ran her hands over his chest. It was hard and smooth, and the feel of it excited her deep down in her belly. She pressed harder against him. She going to regret this. She knew that already. She didn't care. This man was going to break her heart again. But right now, with his arms around her, it was worth it.

One night. Just one night.

She tugged off his sweater, threw it aside, and then dropped kisses across his chest. He pulled away, but only so he could capture her lips in another kiss. He ran one hand over her neck and down her back to her ass, cupping it and pulling her against his length. She gasped at his hardness and wrapped her arms around his neck. Her hips moved back and forth against him as if of their own volition.

She snagged his belt buckle, but he ended the kiss and grabbed her hands, pinning them gently behind her back. He pressed his lips to the pulse point on her neck and then kissed his way down to the hollow before releasing her hands and lifting the hem of her sweater. He glanced up at her for permission, and she nodded. *Oh, hell yes.* The sweater fell to the floor, followed by her bra, and his eyes roamed over her skin. "You are even more beautiful than I remember. I didn't think it was possible."

She looked up at him through her lashes. "You're pretty damn fine yourself." She ran her hands over his chest. "Not a kid anymore, but a man." She sucked one of his nipples, and he groaned.

"You're damn right," he said as he picked her up and lowered her to the bed. He undid her jeans and pulled them down over her hips. Then she reached up and helped him take off his jeans and underwear. He slowly lowered himself on top of her, his weight, his length, pushing against her, and it felt so good. So right. It was as if he was the missing puzzle piece her body had craved.

He kissed her deeply, slowing the pace, then dipped his head to suck her nipple. She moaned when his tongue swirled around the hard bud. She moved her hands to his ass and squeezed, pulling him closer to her core, needing him there. Needing him inside of her. He growled her name, and the husky, desperate sound of it made her heart flutter in her chest.

He bent his head to suck her other nipple, then slowly left a trail of kisses down her stomach to her underwear. She was wearing a lace thong. He cocked an eyebrow. "This is what you wear?" he growled. "All the time?"

She bit her lip and nodded.

He swore. "You are going to be the death of me. I can't unknow this. Now I'm going to be hard whenever you're in the room." His gaze locked with hers. "And even when you're not."

"Hudson," she breathed out, urging him on.

He curled his fingers around the lace and tugged. It gave very quickly, and he dropped the thong to the floor.

He sucked her nipple and then moved lower, his mouth hovering over her center. When he blew a hot breath, she whispered his name, straining her hips to reach him. He dropped a kiss onto her core.

She curled her fingers around the bedsheets as he slid his hands under her hips to bring her to his mouth. He used his tongue to tease and suckle her, taking her to the brink. When he stopped, she couldn't help but cry out. It was even better than she'd imagined, and she'd imagined a lot. He teased her to the brink once more, his tongue dancing over her sweet spot, his fingers driving into her in a steady rhythm, faster and faster until she crashed over the edge, yelling his name as she arched beneath him.

"That was incredible." She tugged him down on top of her. She ran her hands along his back and then pulled his mouth down to hers, claiming it with a ferocity she'd never known she possessed. This man drove her wild, and she wanted him. Inside her. Now.

Their gazes locked as she stroked him. He was hard as rock.

"Wait," he said as he sat up. He dug in his wallet and produced a condom.

She took it from him. "I'll take care of that when I'm ready." She pushed him back down on the bed and straddled him. Raining kisses down his jaw, she ran her hands across his chest, exploring. He groaned when she lowered her mouth to his nipple. She loved that she had the ability to drive this big, powerful man crazy with her touch. It was intoxicating.

She shifted her weight until she was centered over his groin, slowly rubbing her core across his cock. He flexed against her. She wanted him so very badly, and she knew he wanted to be inside her, too.

But she also knew she loved him. She'd never stopped. The puppy love they'd shared back then was blooming into something new and stronger, an emotion that would refuse to be dismissed long after this night became a memory. Part of her thought she should run, but it was too late to run. Even if she left now, her heart would still hurt. So she planned on making the most of the time she had with him. She would deal with the fallout later.

She grabbed the condom and ripped the package open with her teeth. She smiled as she took Hudson's cock in her hand and slowly rolled the condom down. His blue eyes turned indigo.

She raised her hips and moved his cock into place before lowering herself down onto him. The first time, she just let the tip enter her before she pulled back. He swore.

Smiling, she started lowering herself again. This time, she took in more of him. She wanted to tease him for longer, but she couldn't handle it. She *needed* him. Hudson reached out and grabbed her hips, and she rode him, picking up the pace. The feel of him inside her, filling her up, was exquisite.

Her breath was coming in small gasps. She was going to come. She said his name and urged him on, her hips rushing to meet his rhythm, her fingernails raking across his chest as he pounded into her. Nothing had ever felt this good, this right. She was teetering on the brink and had to bite her lip to keep from screaming.

He thrust deep inside her, and she crashed over the edge, euphoria filling her every cell. Hudson followed her, saying her name in his deep sexy growl.

She flopped down onto his chest, and he wrapped both arms around her.

"You never cease to amaze me," he said.

She didn't respond. She was going to enjoy this for as long as she could. Reality would come with the sunrise, and reality hadn't been kind to her lately.

CHAPTER 14

HUDSON PROPPED himself up on the pillows beside Sunny. They were lying side by side with their heads and shoulders touching. "I've missed you, Sunny." He had no idea where the hell that had come from, but the moment it escaped his lips, he knew the truth of it. He'd missed her so much more than he'd let himself admit.

"I've missed you too, Hudson." Sunny sighed. "Life definitely turned out differently than I thought it would."

He nodded. "That's for sure." And, suddenly, the time felt right to do what he should have done when he first saw her at the diner. His gut tensed, but he needed to get the words out. He owed her that much.

"Sunny, I want to apologize for running out on you back in high school. I never meant to hurt you." He chanced a glance at her, but her face was impassive. "I couldn't take it anymore. Dad wanted me to stay and take over the ranch. He applied in my name to an agriculture program, and that night he came to tell me I got in. I lost it. We fought. It was bad. Really bad. He gave me a choice, go to school or be disowned.

"Tunning the ranch was never the life I wanted. You know that. My mom loves the land, and she takes care of it a lot better than Dad. I love it here too, but I never wanted to make it my profession."

Sunny nodded. "I remember what your dad was like. Brutal." He was trying to pick up any signals from her, but her voice was neutral. She would make a hell of a spy.

"I wanted you to know that it had nothing to do with you. I didn't say goodbye face to face because I couldn't. I wouldn't be able to leave you, and I couldn't stay. You were a year behind me in school. You needed to finish high school. I couldn't take you with me. I couldn't offer you anything. I barely had enough money to get to Missoula, let alone take care of the two of us. I knew if I saw you, I would chicken out. I loved you Sunny, but I needed to leave, and it was that night or not at all."

"I get it, Hudson. We were kids. Don't get me wrong, you broke my heart, and your note sucked. 'Dear Sunny, I love you but I have to go. Take Care, Hudson.' Seriously?" she cocked an eyebrow at him. "I deserved better than that, but I understand. We both had some growing up to do, and we had to do it our own way. Still, I wish you'd said something. It messed with my head. It made me think you didn't care about me."

Hudson grabbed her hand and squeezed. "God no. I was so in love with you I couldn't see straight, but there was nothing I could do. Not then."

"I get it now, Hudson. Your mom and I talked about it when I came out to the ranch one day after I got back. She didn't say much. Just that your dad had been a real bastard to you and, in the end, it was better for you to go than to stay. I'm okay with it. I just wanted to hear you say you were sorry, and now you have, so thanks."

He couldn't get the words out. Her forgiveness meant everything to him. He swallowed, hard. "You know, I didn't want to come back. I love the ranch, but I've always had bad memories about the way I left. You were the only good thing about Canyon Springs in my mind. You still are. Canyon Springs will always be where I'm from, and I love being back, but you make it home."

He swallowed. He owed her another apology. "I need to tell you something else."

She looked at him and then pulled her hand from his. "What is it?" she asked in a flat voice.

"Your lawyer, Vince, didn't hire me. That is, he did but not the way you think. Hank is a friend so I had him call Vince and offer my services pro bono. I knew things were bad, and I wanted to be able to protect you, but I knew you wouldn't let me if I offered. So I—"

"Went behind my back and manipulated me." Sunny hopped up out of the bed and jerked the sheet with her, wrapping it around herself. "You are a colossal asshole. Do you know that? I was doing fine on my own. Nobody shot at me before you were here. Maybe it's you they're shooting at! Where do you get off lying to me and treating me like a child?! Are you for real?"

"I didn't mean to. I wanted to help because I felt guilty—"

"You're helping me because you feel guilty? That's worse! What, I'm some poor lost little girl who can't manage anything without you? Hudson to the rescue."

Hudson stood up slowly. "That's not what I—"

"Listen up, asshat! I left town just after high school graduation. I went to Cornell, which has the number one hospitality program in the country! Then I moved to L.A., and I worked my way up to event manager at the Jasmine Door Hotel in Beverly Hills, one of *the* top hotel chains in the world! As a matter of fact, I was offered the same position in Macau because there were some major issues there, and the owner, Jameson Drake, wanted *me* to fix them. I would have been in Macau by now if my grandmother hadn't gotten sick."

She held her sheet with one hand and pointed at Hudson with the other. "And just so you know, I've traveled the world plenty on my own. I've been to London, Paris, and Rome. I've been to Australia and Greece. I've been all over the place. The only place I haven't been that was on our list is Giraffe Manor in Kenya. I was booked to go before all this happened! So save your fucking guilt and pity. I don't need rescuing, thank you very much! Especially by you! I can take care of myself. So back off and leave me the hell alone." She pointed to the door. "Get out!"

Hudson clenched his jaw. He grabbed his clothes and pulled on his underwear. He opened the bedroom door and slammed it behind him. He hadn't meant it like that. Fuck. She was twisting his words. He'd wanted her to know that he cared, that he was worried about her and wanted to help. Rhys had been right. This was one big clusterfuck.

CHAPTER 15

SUNNY PETTED HUCK'S head as she sat on the front porch. The ranch looked beautiful in the afternoon sun—majestic mountains rising behind the rolling fields and soft hills.

She took a sip of her tea and shivered slightly. It had been a cold, lonely day, and she missed her grandmother and her own bed. The bed here felt like a traitor since she could still smell Hudson's scent on her pillow even though she'd changed the sheets. And despite everything, it gave her a pang of longing.

The screen door whined, and a few seconds later, a blanket descended around her shoulders. She looked up to see Rhys standing there.

"Thanks, Rhys," she said as she leaned forward and wrapped herself in the old multicolored granny square afghan. "Haven't seen much of you today." She hadn't seen anyone except the occasional ranch hand.

It was like she was living in solitary confinement already.

Rhys patted Huck's head and gave him a quick scratch behind the ears before sitting down on the chair next to hers. "I had another doctor's appointment early this morning, and then I spent the day wandering around town."

Sunny glanced at his leg. She'd noticed his limp seemed a bit better than it had last night. "Wait, you spent the day in town? It's not that big. What did you look at?"

Rhys smiled. "Well, I checked out the shops on main street. The local coffee shop is an interesting mix. Very hipster meets rancher."

"That pretty much sums up the whole town. It's changed a lot since we grew up. More hipsters and fewer ranchers. With Missoula just down the road, we attract an eclectic crowd. When Gran first told me about the coffee shop, I worried the diner might be in trouble, but we've made enough changes that the hipster crowd has embraced the diner as well. It's a very live and let live group." She frowned. "Usually, anyway."

"This will all be over soon."

Sunny bit her lip. "The neighbors I've known all my life have suddenly...turned on me. Even if my name is miraculously cleared, this won't all go away. Now someone's trying to kill me, and I have no idea who's after me or why."

"Fear makes people do funny things. That's not an excuse for how they're treating you. Just an explanation. As for who's trying to kill you, I can honestly say I have no idea."

She took a sip of tea. "So what else did you see in town?"

Rhys crossed his boot-clad feet out in front of him. "The high-end designer shops mixed in with the feed stores and such was a weird combo for sure. The Canyon Springs Brewery was nice, though."

Sunny chuckled. "Yes, they have some good microbrews. They also have an awesome steak sandwich."

Rhys grinned. "I did notice that."

"So I guess you won't want any of the chili I made for supper," Sunny teased.

"I wouldn't go that far. Lunch was a while ago." He patted his flat belly. "I can always eat. What did you do today besides make chili?"

Sunny shrugged. "Nothing. I slept late, which was nice for a change." She'd slept late cause she'd been up tossing and turning all night, trying to keep from killing Hudson. "Read a little bit, and I brought Peanut some carrots down at the stables. She saved my hide. It seemed like the least I could do."

"Hudson been around?"

Hearing his name almost made her flinch.

"I haven't seen him," she said coolly. "He was gone when I got up. But he did leave me a note saying he'd be working around the ranch today and I'd be perfectly safe because of the security system and the ranch hands."

She wasn't sure if she was happy he wasn't around or angry. She hated that he'd lied to her, but he'd made her feel safe and loved. It was something she so desperately craved at the moment. She'd been craving Hudson's touch for a long time.

She swore silently. She was done with Hudson Riggs. She just had to remind herself of that fact every minute or so.

She sighed. It was probably for the best that he was ignoring her. They'd had mind-blowing sex, and she'd been a more than willing participant, even knowing it might be only the one time. But it had taken all of two minutes for their bliss to devolve into a bitter argument. She needed to let it all go. She and Hudson weren't a good combination, at least outside of the bedroom.

She cleared her throat and took another sip of her now cold tea.

"He's right," Rhys said. "You're fine so long as you stay here. There are plenty of security measures."

She made a non-committal noise in her throat and then glanced at her watch. "It's dinner time and I, for one, am starving." Huck lifted his head and looked at her hopefully. "Apparently Huck feels the same way." The dog's tail started thumping the porch in agreement. "Okay, boy, let's get you fed."

When she stood, Huck practically leapt to his feet. He gave a big stretch before he went over to the screen door and batted it with his paw. She laughed. "Come on, Rhys, let's go feed the mutt."

Rhys stood up. "I'll text Hudson and let him know we're eating."

Sunny didn't bother to reply. What was the point? She opened the door and headed straight back to the kitchen.

Rhys walked in as she was getting the salad out of the fridge. "Hudson said to go ahead without him."

"Okay, thanks." She shot Rhys a brittle smile. He probably knew it was fake, but so be it. She was tired of pretending to be okay. She wanted all of this to be over. The murder charges. Hudson. Everything. It felt like her life was out of her control. She tried to swallow a sob, but a gasping noise escaped, almost like she was drowning. And, oh, she *felt* like she was drowning.

"You okay over there? Need some help?" Rhys was standing in the middle of the kitchen, eyebrows raised.

"I'm fine. My hand still hurts a little is all."

Rhys nodded. "Can you grab the cucumber yoghurt salad, too? I developed a taste for it in the middle east. Along with tzatziki sauce."

She set the first salad on the kitchen table and went back to the fridge for the other one. She placed that on the table, too, and then grabbed some bowls.

Her mind was whirring, her feelings churning. Working on autopilot, she ladled chili into the bowls. As she poured the last spoonful into the bowl, something clicked. She froze. Could it be? She knew she could confirm it, but she had to get to the diner.

She made a quick decision. "I need to run into town later and grab some...work stuff from the diner. I'll be climbing the walls soon if I don't find something to do."

Rhys sat down at the table, and Sunny brought over the bowls and some plates for the salad. He quietly placed a napkin next to her bowl. "Why don't you wait 'til Hudson gets back?"

"It's a quick ride into town. I have no intention of interacting with anyone other than the people who work at the diner, and they've all been sweet to me. I can bring you or one of the other men."

"I hear what you're saying, but it's up to Hudson to decide if it's safe." Rhys picked up his spoon and took a bite of chili. "This is good by the way."

Sunny mentally rolled her eyes. *Hudson's been gone all day, but he gets to decide what's safe?* "Thanks." Besides, if she was right, this could change everything.

Rhys put down his spoon. "Look, despite what you might think, Hudson takes his work very seriously. If he's not around, it's 'cause he knows you'll be safe here. He's not going to do anything that would put you in any kind of danger. You can count on him to keep you safe, but you have to do what he says."

Sunny gave Rhys a nod and a tight smile as she chewed her food, but she was having trouble swallowing. *Hudson takes his work very seriously.* She hadn't thought about it much, but maybe she was just a job to Hudson. He'd said as much last night. He'd offered his services for free because he felt guilty about leaving in high school. And, hey, if she wanted to crawl into bed with him...well hell, why not? She'd been such an idiot. Time to put the past behind her permanently. She needed to put on her big girl panties and get on with life.

After dinner, Rhys offered to help her with the dishes, but she sent him away. She looked for him after she finished and found him sound asleep on the sofa in the great room. All that walking must have done him in. She'd seen him rub his leg during dinner. The body always needed lots of rest to recover properly, or so she'd been told.

Hudson still wasn't back. She could wait, but this was too important. The sooner she knew the truth, the better it would be for her and Gran. Plus, she needed to prove to herself that she wasn't afraid. That whoever had shot at her hadn't taken her spine and her spirit with them. She walked back into the kitchen and saw the keys to Hudson's mother's pickup hanging from the hook.

Decision made, she ran upstairs to grab her

purse. When she came back down, she took the keys. She wouldn't talk to anyone except for the night staff at the diner, and no one would know she was the one in Hudson's mom's truck. It would be fine.

And it was. At least leaving the ranch was. She gave a little wave to the man at the gate, hoping he wouldn't look too closely, and he didn't.

Thoughts churned in her head. Wayne. The killer. Hudson. It was all so much. Sunny felt a tug on the wheel. Her heart leapt in her throat. The front tire almost dropped off the road as she rounded Dead Man's Curve. A shudder wracked her spine. It was a long way down on either side. She focused on her driving the rest of the way into town. Within minutes, she was in downtown Canyon Springs, and it was a damn good thing because her heart was hammering so hard in her chest she thought it would pop right out

It felt so strange to see all the people out on the sidewalks—chatting, laughing, having fun. A pang of envy struck her heart. It felt like years since she had been one of those people. She missed California and her friends so much. The last six months in Canyon Springs had been more difficult that she'd ever imagined.

She pulled into the parking lot behind the diner and stopped in front of the back door. She wiped her palms on her jeans. After glancing around to see if anyone was watching, she hopped out of the truck and hurried through the door.

"Hey, Marc," she called to the late-shift cook as she entered. "How are things going tonight?"

He gave her a big smile. "Hey, Sunny. Doing good. Business is swift. Just the way I like it."

She smiled back. "I'm here to grab some paperwork."

He nodded and got back to flipping burgers. Sunny went to her bookcase and grabbed a pile of papers and then sat down at her desk. It only took a few minutes for Sunny to find what she needed. They kept the orders for a month. She pulled out Wayne's order. It confirmed her suspicions. She tucked the order in her pocket and headed back into the kitchen. "Have a good night, Marc."

He nodded and waved.

Sunny hopped back into the truck. Within minutes, she was back on the highway out of town. "See, no sweat," she mumbled to herself. She didn't need Hudson or anyone else standing guard all the time. She just needed to be smart.

She leaned back in her seat and kept her hands loose on the steering wheel, tried to relax and enjoy the ride. It was a nice night. The sky was clear, there were stars for miles, and she was the only one on the road. But her brain kept working the problem.

A burger and fries. That was the key. Wayne didn't eat gluten. He didn't even eat much meat. He'd made a big point of bragging about his healthy habits after finding out she used to live in L.A. So why had he ordered a cheeseburger platter in addition to his salad? Because someone else was with him. She thought back to that night. Although she'd seen nothing to indicate he wasn't alone, Wayne *had* acted a little funny. He'd sort of rushed her off and made no attempt to hit on her.

Her thoughts were moving too fast. She needed to calm down. She took a deep breath and let it out. Then again. And again. Her shoulders finally dropped a little, and some of her nervous energy seeped away. She realized she was craving something sweet. She should've gotten some apple pie from Marc, or maybe she could keep driving and go over to Missoula and grab some desert. Maybe keep going from there. She could be back in L.A. in no time.

A glare hit her eyes as headlights popped up in her rearview mirror. The car behind her had their high beams on. She tilted the mirror a bit and then glanced in the side mirror. The headlights were a lot closer.

"Someone's in a hurry," she murmured. She glanced down at the speedometer. She was doing slightly over the speed limit. Whoever it was could go around her if they were in that much of a hurry. She was not speeding up.

She checked the rearview mirror again. The vehicle behind her looked like some sort of SUV. It was the same height as hers and way too close for comfort. *An out-of-towner? Some teenager going too fast?* A shiver went down her back, but she was determined not to panic. Panicking would only put her in more danger.

The SUV behind her came closer still. Her palms were slick with sweat as her gaze went from the road to her mirrors to the road again. It was wide open, and there were dotted lines coming up. Maybe they were just getting ready to pass?

The dotted lines came and went. The SUV stayed behind her, mere inches from her bumper. She glanced over to the passenger seat, but her purse was too far away for her to reach her cell.

Suddenly her truck jolted and Sunny screamed. She gripped the wheel hard, trying to keep the big pickup on the road. The truck rammed her again, harder this time. Her seatbelt held her in place, but she jerked the wheel accidentally and veered out of her lane.

Her heart thumping wildly in her chest, she tried to figure out what to do. Dead Man's Curve was coming up in a few miles, and there was a nasty drop on her side of the road. If he hit her there, she would go off for sure. She looked in the mirror, but the SUV had dropped back. It was slowing down, and the headlights were getting smaller.

Sunny sagged with relief. Whoever it was stopped. Maybe they'd realized they were playing a dangerous game. Maybe it had been another kid trying to torment her...not hurt her. Either way, Sunny wanted to get back to the ranch. Another glance in the review mirror revealed the lights were gone.

Sunny slumped and eased her grip on the wheel. Maybe music would help. Her hand shook as she hit the button for the radio. An ad for a local restaurant came blaring through the speakers. Something about hamburgers. Sunny hit the button to turn it off again. She put her hand over her heart. Dear God, she did *not* need any more scares tonight.

The cheeseburger platter. The last piece of the puzzle clicked into place. She knew now who had been with Wayne when he died, but what did that prove? And how was she going to get people to believe her?

Her truck suddenly jolted forward and Sunny screamed. She wrestled with the wheel to keep the pickup under control. The SUV was back, only this time the lights were off. She braced for a second hit. The SUV pulled around as if to pass her and hit her back tire dead center. Sunny fought with the wheel, but the GMC turned sideways. The other driver hit the brights, and she was temporarily blinded as the SUV crashed into the side of the pickup again, pushing her. She looked out the passenger side window and saw...nothing. She was in Dead Man's Curve.

The pickup lost its grip on the road and vaulted over the guardrail. It rolled over again and again. Sunny lost track of how many times. The cacophony of shattering glass and bending metal was deafening. It seemed to last forever. And then sudden silence. Sunny tried to focus, to keep her eyes open, but everything was just one big blur.

CHAPTER 16

SUNNY SQUEEZED HER EYES SHUT. Nothing made sense. She slowly raised her eyelids. Her vision cleared, but it took a second for her brain to grasp her situation. There was a cloud hanging in front of her face. The airbag. She could just see over it.

The truck's headlights lit up tree trunks, but they were all upside down. How did the trees get upside down? Her vision swam again but cleared after a second. She squinted and tried to focus.

It wasn't the trees. *She* was upside down with her arms hanging above her head. She tried to move them, but they were too weak. She focused and tried again. Success. She moved the airbag out of the way and tried to take stock.

Her head hurt. She probably had a concussion. When she touched her hairline, her fingers came back sticky. But at least all of her fingers moved. She had no back pain, but her ribs and shoulder hurt. Her hips hurt a bit, too, but her legs and toes all moved.

She blinked again. Her headache was getting worse, probably because of the blood rushing to her head. She wanted out, but if she unbuckled her seatbelt, she'd drop onto her head. A quick search revealed there was nothing soft to land on. Her purse seemed to be missing, along with her cell phone.

Every window in the truck had shattered, and the safety glass lay all over the floor, but not much else. Sunny shivered. Time to get out. She put one hand down to break her fall and found the seat belt buckle again with the other. She took a deep breath and hit the button. Her bracing hand didn't hold her, but the maneuver saved her head—she was able to turn and land on her side.

Sunny lay there for a moment, giving herself a chance to breathe and gather her wits. A few deep breaths later, she realized she could smell gas. Panic started crawling up her throat. What if the truck blew up?

The thought galvanized Sunny, and she managed to crawl out of the driver's side window, but it took all of her remaining strength. She lay beside the truck for a moment to rest and catch her breath. The truck had turned so it was perpendicular to the road. The headlights faced the trees and the back was wedged against an embankment.

She was so damn tired. Maybe she could just stay

here for a minute. Her eyes started to close, but she was jolted awake by the sound of rocks falling. Was someone coming to help her? She looked up the embankment, but it was pitch black. More rocks falling. Maybe she should call out so whoever it was could help her. She opened her mouth to yell, but another thought popped into head. What if it was the person who'd tried to kill her?

Icy fingers gripped her heart, and for a moment she was frozen, fear immobilizing her muscles. More cascading rocks. It was the sound of shuffling feet that finally pushed Sunny into action. She looked around. The headlights had dimmed so it was hard to see, but she could tell she was at the bottom of the embankment, surrounded by trees. She half crawled half dragged herself off to the right, feeling the way with her hands.

The foot falls stopped so Sunny stopped, too. She did not want the person to hear her until she was sure the coast was clear. More falling rocks. She started crawling toward the trees again, moving as quickly and quietly as her injuries would allow. She was about fifteen feet away from the truck when a flashlight clicked on partway down the embankment. The darkness around her was so complete that the beam provided some weak light for her, too. She ducked behind a tree, waited a beat, and then peeked around the trunk.

The man had finally made it down the embankment and was working his way around to the driver's door of the truck. He crouched down and shone his flashlight inside the cab before turning away from the truck. Sunny stayed as still as possible as he shone his flashlight over the trees.

"Sunny? Sunny are you here?"

Sunny recognized the voice right away. She almost sobbed with relief. Colin Edwards had found her. She started to move and then stopped. She frowned. Why wasn't his radio on? Shouldn't he be calling this in and asking for help? Sunny looked up the embankment. Why weren't his red and blue lights flashing? Surely, she would see them if they were on. Maybe he had his personal car?

"Sunny?" he called again. She peeked around the tree trunk and saw Colin outlined in the pickup's headlights. He was in uniform, but that wasn't what made her gasp. He was holding his gun.

CHAPTER 17

"Fuck!" Hudson roared as he slammed the steering wheel with his hand. "How could you let her go off on her own?"

"I didn't let her do jack," Rhys growled back through the Bluetooth connection. Hudson had called to check in on her on his way home, only to find out she wasn't there. "I told her not to leave without checking with you," Rhys continued. "She agreed. I had no idea she was going to do this."

Hudson ran a hand through his hair. "Sorry, man. It's my fault. I should've known better than to leave her on her own all day. She's never been good at doing nothing."

"Rhys said. "I really didn't think she'd leave. I… took a pain pill at dinner. It made me fall asleep."

"There's no shame in that. You got shot. You need

time to recover. Walking all over town today probably wasn't the best idea."

"How did you know I was in town?" Rhys asked.

Hudson sighed. "Look, I know I said I was going to be on the ranch, working out in the pastures, but I got out there and just couldn't do it. I took the ranch truck into town and saw you. I spent the day asking questions, trying to track down Sunny's harassers."

"And did you?"

"The high school football team is pissed because Wayne had made such a fuss about helping them. They decided to harass her as revenge. When did Sunny leave?"

Rhys sighed. "I honestly don't know. Do you want me to check the cameras?"

"No. I'm gonna pull off the road and make a few calls. I'll keep in touch. If she shows up, let me know ASAP."

"Will do. Hudson, I'm sorry. I should've—"

"No. This isn't on you. It's on me. You're on vacation." He clicked off the call so Rhys wouldn't try to argue. After firing off a couple of texts to the ranch hands he had working security, he tried Sunny's cell. It went straight to voicemail. His gut churned. Was she okay? What if she wasn't?

No, he wasn't going down that road. Not yet.

He hit the steering wheel again, pissed, but not at Rhys. He'd promised to protect Sunny, but he'd failed —all because he'd gone off on his own to solve the mystery of who was harassing her, hoping that maybe she'd forgive him for being such an asshole and give him a second chance.

No, third chance. Did he even want that? He was only in town until his mom came back from Florida. After that, he'd be back in Amman at Black Thorn headquarters. It was stupid to even entertain the idea of picking up again with Sunny but, goddammit, he wanted her!

His cell rang. Rhys's name showed up on the screen.

"What?" he barked.

"I spoke with Marc at the diner. Sunny left at least a half hour ago. He said she was in and out in a hurry, didn't mention anything about stopping anywhere else."

"Shit!" She should have been back at the ranch by now. "Okay. I'm heading home along the route she would've taken from town. It's gonna take me probably twenty minutes to get back. I was out at the Lawson place, talking to the current high school quarterback. Are you okay to move?"

Rhys snorted. "What do you need?"

"Take the main road into town. Yell if you find her first."

"On it," Rhys said. "I'll call you from the road."

Hudson ended the call as he swerved around a downed branch. The wind had picked up, and clouds now rolled and covered the moon. He pressed down on the accelerator. Twenty minutes was too long, but he wasn't sure the vehicle he was in could go beyond the speed limit. He was going to push it anyway.

He took the turn to bypass town. It was slightly longer, but it would be quicker than inching through town. He grabbed his cell off the seat next to him and hit a couple of buttons.

"Patterson," said the voice over the truck speakers.

"Hank, it's Hudson. I need some help. Sunny took off tonight, and I'm trying to locate her. Can you ping her cell?"

In his usual brusque way, Hank didn't stop to ask what had happened but just said, "Yes. Give me her number."

Hudson rattled off her digits.

"I'll need a couple minutes. Call you back."

Hudson clicked off and cursed. The night was so dark it was hard to see anything out the windows. What the hell had she been thinking? What was so important it couldn't wait until the morning? His cell rang again.

"Riggs."

"She's pinging along 318 on Dead Man's Curve. I'm tracking your cell, too. I'll keep watch from this end. Let me know if you need anything else. I'll have medivac on standby just in case."

"Thanks, Hank," Hudson said, but Hank Patterson had already hung up.

Medivac. The pain in his chest was excruciating.

If Sunny needed a medivac... No, he couldn't think of her being hurt. Dead Man's Curve had claimed way too many lives. Sunny's would not be one of them.

He hit the accelerator again, pouring his concentration into staying on the road and getting there as fast as possible. He couldn't deal with the fears in his head. He needed Sunny to be fine.

The curve snuck up on him, and he hit the brakes. The back of the pickup shuddered and slid a bit, but he kept it under control. He hit the button on his cell. Rhys's voice came through the speakers. "I just hit Dead Man's Curve."

"Yeah, me, too," Hudson responded. "Go slow and keep your eyes peeled. Stay on the line in case you spot something."

"Agreed."

Hudson slowed to a crawl. He looked over the edge, but it was a yawning emptiness, the night too dark for him to see anything. He would have to walk the curve with a flashlight. He relayed his new strategy to Rhys.

Hudson parked the truck. He left on his four-way flashers and high beams to provide extra light and grabbed his flashlight out of the glove box before he climbed out of the truck. He walked to the edge and shone his flashlight down the embankment. Nothing but trees. He started walking, swinging his flashlight back and forth, keeping his eyes on the road.

Two minutes later, fear shot down his spine. Skid

marks. They went sideways and then over the embankment. Sunny. Hudson started running toward the edge. He couldn't breathe. His body was working on muscle memory because his brain had stopped functioning. He reached the edge and shone his light over. There, about sixty feet down, was his mom's pickup lying upside down.

CHAPTER 18

SUNNY'S KNEES started to give out. She clung to the tree bark in terror. What was she going to do? Her chest was on fire.

Breathe. She gulped air.

Colin couldn't see her. Should she keep still or try to move parallel to the embankment? The road flattened out after Dead Man's Curve. If she kept walking, she could reach a point where she could flag down help.

Who was she kidding? It was so damn dark she couldn't see more than a foot in front of her face. She was stuck.

She wished she'd worn a watch. How long had she been out here? Surely, Hudson would know she was missing by now. Or maybe not. What if he was still out somewhere and Rhys was still asleep? Nausea rose in her throat.

"Sunny?" Colin called again. "I know you're here. You didn't have time to get far, and it's pitch black so you can't see much."

He was right. She'd never make it to the end of the embankment in the dark. Not without running face-first into a tree. She closed her eyes and prayed like she'd never prayed before.

"Look, I need you to come out. I promise it'll be quick."

A sob escaped her lips. She saw the beam of the flashlight bounce around in the trees to her right.

"I'm sorry, Sunny. You were always nice to me, even back in high school. I want you to know I didn't set you up to take the fall on purpose. You left your scarf behind. It wasn't personal or anything."

Not personal? Sunny wanted to scream. It felt pretty damn personal to her! Her knees trembled. Tears ran silently down her face.

"I promise I'll look in on Clara for you. She's a nice lady, your gran. She'll be okay."

Gran! Her heart pounded in her ears, and her vision clouded. She didn't want him anywhere near her grandmother. She seethed at the thought of him going to Gran, acting sympathetic. No. She wasn't going to let that happen. Not without a fight.

The flashlight beam danced to her left this time, along the embankment. She heard Colin take a couple of steps.

"I didn't want to kill you but, you know, you

started asking questions. I couldn't take the risk, Sunny. If you'd just kept your head down and kept your boyfriend on a leash, this wouldn't be happening. I would have made sure you got off on a technicality.

"I was going to make a mistake. Lose evidence. People would have been upset, even the chief, but you know what? They would've understood. They would've thought I was trying to help you and Clara. It all would've worked out, but not now. Too many people asking too many questions."

The flashlight beam was bouncing from tree to tree. "You're starting to piss me off, Sunny. I'm usually a patient man, but this whole situation has me a bit on edge."

Piss *him* off? Sunny looked down at her feet, searching for anything she could use as a weapon. But it was still too dark to see, so she crouched to the ground and started feeling around with her hands. Nothing but leaves, twigs, and what felt like a beer bottle. She briefly considered the bottle, but she'd have to get way too close to Colin to use that.

She slowly got down on her belly and stretched out her arms. She hoped the brush was thick enough to cover her. She shivered. It was cold, and the ground was damp. But she moved slowly, her hands reaching outward in attempt to find something, anything she could use.

Then her fingers finally glanced off a branch. Not

too small. It had some heft to it. Sunny tugged it gently, and it moved. She guessed that it was a couple of inches thick and about two and a half feet long. She wanted to jump for joy.

Now all she had to do was pick it up and get to her feet without being noticed. *Oh, and smack Colin with the stick when he came close. Which he will have no reason to do because he can shoot you.*

She'd brought a branch to a gun fight. Nervous laughter fought to come out, but she bit her tongue to control it.

Colin took a few more steps in her general direction. "Suunny," he called. Then there was another sound, much farther off. A car maybe? Oh, God, maybe they would see Colin's car and stop. Hope blossomed in her chest.

Colin must have heard it, too, because he switched off the light. Sunny took the opportunity to grab the stick and popped upright, returning to her position behind the tree.

The flashlight came back on. "I know what you're thinking, Sunny, but I parked my truck off the road. No one will see it."

Sunny wanted to scream. Dread filled her belly. Colin was getting closer, and she had no idea if the stick would be large enough or heavy enough to knock the gun out of his hand. Even if it did, he was much larger than her and she was injured. There was little chance she'd be able to get away from him. But that's all she needed: a little chance.

She remembered the bottle. Holding her breath, she slowly inched down again and found it. Picked it up. Then she stood up again and waited for her moment. The flashlight bobbed among the trees to her right, but this time his search seemed more systematic. Colin was moving from tree to tree, coming closer to her position. If he took a few more steps, he would be able to see her, but she wouldn't be close enough to hit him.

Then there was another sound. A cascade of rock. Was someone coming?

Colin swung the flashlight around to the embankment. Sensing her chance, she snuck a quick peek around the tree trunk. Sure enough, Colin was running the flashlight beam over the embankment. She turned and went around the other side of the tree and threw the bottle as far as she could. It landed with a thunk on the other side of the downed truck.

Colin shifted the light again, and as soon as his back was to Sunny, she picked up the branch and quietly stepped out from behind the tree. She swung for all she was worth and hit Colin directly on the back of the head. He dropped the flashlight and went down like a stone.

Sunny scrambled as quickly as she could up the embankment. She kept losing her footing and sliding back. Her hands were getting cut up, but she refused to give up. A hand grabbed her ankle when she was about halfway up. She screamed at the top of her lungs. Colin had her. She kicked at him, but he grabbed her other foot and started pulling her back down. She screamed again. Suddenly, the whole area was lit up.

Colin froze.

"Let her go or I swear to God I will blow your head off."

Sunny looked up, but she was blinded by the floodlights. It took a second for her eyes to adjust. Still, she would recognize that voice anywhere. Hudson had come for her, and there were men all along the top of the embankment with shotguns pointed in their general direction. Ranch hands. Hudson was holding a handgun aimed at Colin's head.

"You got him?" he asked.

"Affirmative," Rhys responded.

Hudson tucked the gun in his belt and moved down the embankment toward Sunny.

She had never been so happy to see anyone in her entire life. She looked down at Colin. He still had her ankles in a firm grip. A flash of something crossed his face, and she knew what he was thinking. She kicked as hard as she could. He wasn't going to hold her hostage. No way. She got one foot free and slammed him in the face. He fell backward, sliding partway down the embankment.

Hudson reached down and grabbed Sunny by the arms. "Jesus, you're gonna be the death of me." He pulled her to her feet and helped her up the rest of the way.

When they reached the top, cop cars were arriving in droves. Lights flashed; sirens blared. There was even an ambulance parking just down the way. Sunny turned to Hudson. "Thank—"

He grabbed her and crushed her to his chest. She wrapped her arms around him and squeezed him back. Tears started down her cheeks. "Oh, God," she sobbed. He was holding her so tightly she was having trouble breathing, but she wasn't about to complain. If he let go, she'd be on the ground. She had no ability to stand without him.

"Sunny, you scared the hell out of me," he whispered in her ear. "A man can only take so much. Don't you ever do that to me again."

"Scared *you*?" she mumbled. "I was terrified." She tried to pull back, but Hudson kept his arms locked around her. She looked up into his face. "Thanks for coming to get me. I...I owe you an apology. I'm so sorry about your mom's truck. I promise I'll replace it."

He stared at her, dumbfounded. "I don't care about the truck. I only care about you. I love you, Sunny. I'm never gonna let you go ever again."

Sunny blinked. Had she heard him right? Her

brain couldn't seem to function. She opened her mouth, but no words came out.

"Ms. Travers? I'm gonna need to speak to you."

"What?" Sunny looked over at Chief Wells in bafflement.

"I need to talk to you about what happened here." The chief was standing next to them, looking as pissed off as she'd ever seen him. What did *he* think had happened here?

"Actually, you don't," Hudson said. "Sunny needs to get checked out by the EMTs, and then she'll provide a statement to Sheriff Striker." Hudson tipped his head toward the man walking in their direction.

"Riggs." The big man in the sheriff's uniform nodded to him. "Ms. Travers, I'm Bill Striker. I'm going to be looking into what happened here tonight. I'm so sorry you had to go through this. How are you feeling?"

Sunny just nodded. She was starting to hurt all over, and her head was pounding.

Striker looked at Hudson. "How about you take her over and let the EMTs take a look at her?"

Hudson nodded.

"Now, wait just one minute," Chief Wells said. "This is *my* crime scene. I'm in charge of the investigation."

"Not anymore," Striker said. "You're about to get a call from the governor. He's asked me to take over.

Election year for him. He can't have the corrupt officer's own police department investigating the case."

As if by clockwork, the chief's cell rang.

Hudson finally loosened his grip on Sunny, but he
kept one arm around her shoulders. She tried to
move, but her legs wouldn't work. Without a word,
Hudson scooped her up and carried her over to the
ambulance. She would have been mortified if she had
any energy at all.

"Can you call Gran?" she asked Hudson once she
was lying on the gurney in the ambulance.

"Already done. She's gonna meet you at the
hospital."

"Okay. That's good," Sunny mumbled before
everything went black again.

CHAPTER 19

SUNNY OPENED HER EYES. The first thing she noticed was the sunlight streaming into her hospital room. The second was that Hudson sat in the chair pushed up against her bed.

"Hey, honey, how are you feelin'?" he asked.

His voice was husky, and there were worry lines etched into the skin around his eyes. He hadn't left her. He'd promised to stay with her last night, and he had.

She smiled. "I'm okay." Her throat was desert dry. "Water?" she croaked.

"Sure." Hudson brought the bed into a sitting position and then swung the attached tray over. There was already a cup of water with a straw, plus a pitcher filled to the brim.

Sunny took a small, exploratory sip, then gulped half of the cup down. The water was heavenly going down her throat. "Thanks," she said, putting it down." I needed that."

Hudson leaned over and hooked a lock of hair behind her ear. "How's the pain? The doctor said you have a concussion and some pretty fierce bruises, but no broken bones."

"She told me the same last night. I won't lie, it hurts, but it's not too bad. Of course, that could be the pain meds talking." She smiled. "The doc said I'll have a hell of a bruise from my shoulder across to my hip from the seatbelt, but I can live with that."

"Me, too." Hudson sat down on the bed beside her and took her hand in both of his. "Sunny, you scared the shit out of me last night. When I saw that truck…" He swallowed, and his eyes got wet.

Her heart skipped a beat. "I'm so sorry I didn't listen to you. I should've stayed at the ranch."

"Yes, you should've, but it's my fault for leaving you alone." He smiled. "You can't stand to sit around doing nothin'. You never could. And it doesn't matter now because it's over and I'm not leaving you again."

Sunny didn't say anything. He'd told her that he loved her last night, but she didn't trust it. Emotions were running high, and he might have gotten caught up in the moment. He might have tripped ahead of himself. She'd been disappointed by him before. She wasn't prepared to put all her eggs in that basket again.

A knock on the door startled her, but it was only

Rhys. "Hey, Sunny. Good to see you with a bit of color in your cheeks. How are you feeling?" he came up to the other side of her bed.

"Better. Much better."

"Good drugs are worth their weight in gold."

Sunny laughed and nodded.

"The sheriff wants to talk to you," Rhys said. "Are you okay with that?"

Sunny nodded, and he went back over to the door and waved. Sheriff Striker walked in and stood at the foot of her bed. He was older than Sunny had realized, but he had the physique of a younger man and a head full of short white hair. His ice blue eyes were intense, and she had no doubt that many criminals had confessed to their crimes under this man's questioning.

"Morning, Ms. Travers. How are you feeling? Are you up to answering some questions?"

"Morning, Sheriff. I'm doing much better than I was last night." Hudson stood up, but he didn't relinquish her hand. Rhys stood on her other side. She had two guard dogs watching over her, and she couldn't have appreciated it more. "What do you need to know?"

"I think we've got an idea of last night's events, but I'd like it if you could run me through what happened." Striker pulled out a pen and a pad of paper.

Sunny grabbed the cup and took another sip of

water. Then she told him her story, ending with the moment Colin had tried to tug her down by the ankles. Hudson squeezed her hand.

"You were very brave." Striker smiled. "I have to say, I'm impressed with your beer bottle trick. I wondered how you got him to turn around."

Sunny smiled back. "It was dumb luck, but it worked."

"So what happens now?" Hudson asked.

"Well, Edwards has been arrested for attempted murder of Ms. Travers. We're gathering evidence to link him to Wayne Bradley's murder, but"—the sheriff shook his head—"we can't figure out motive."

"Sheriff Striker. Colin Edwards killed Wayne Bradley because of Kendra, his wife."

Striker cocked his head. "Ah, Ms. Travers, maybe you can explain that a little."

"Please call me Sunny. I realized last night that Wayne was a health nut. He didn't eat gluten. There's no way he ordered a burger and fries for himself. I know Chief Wells's theory was that I stayed and ate dinner with Wayne, but I couldn't figure out why he was so sure it was *me*. I mean, yes, I know my scarf was there and I've never denied being there, but if Wayne did have dinner with someone else, it could've been anybody. Then it hit me. Tzatziki sauce."

Striker blinked and looked at Rhys then Hudson. Both men shrugged. Striker frowned. "I'm not following."

"I like tzatziki sauce with my fries. It's so much better than ketchup. Tzatziki sauce was part of Wayne's order."

Striker frowned. "I can confirm there was tzatziki sauce found at the scene, but I'm still not following you."

Sunny took a sip of water. "There's only one other person in town who always asks for tzatziki sauce with her fries. Kendra Edwards."

"Son of a bitch," Hudson mumbled. Sunny looked up. The light in his eyes told Sunny that he understood where she was going with this.

"Why would Kendra Edwards be at Wayne Bradley's? And why would Colin kill him over that?" the sheriff asked.

"Kendra and Wayne dated toward the end of high school. Kendra's people didn't have much money, and the scholarship she got for college wasn't enough to pay for everything. But she was determined to leave town and make her mark on the world. Something changed right after graduation. Wayne left, and Kendra stayed behind. I think he decided she was holding him back. He was going to be a big football star. He didn't want a girlfriend to tie him down.

"Anyway, a couple of months later, Kendra's mom passed away, and she had to stay to help with her younger siblings. She never left, and she ended up marrying Colin.

"I'm not sure what happened recently, but there've

been rumors that Wayne was seeing someone before he died. Of course, the chief said it was me, but I think it was Kendra. She's always been so desperate to get out of here. I think she figured Wayne might still be her ticket to moving up in life. I don't know, but my guess is Colin thought he was losing his wife."

She frowned as a wave of sadness washed over her. Although there was no excuse for murder. She hated to think Kendra had felt she had no choice but to go back to the man who'd hurt her.

Sheriff Striker stood there assessing Sunny for a long moment. Finally, he said, "Well, it's a good theory. Turns out Bradley was out of money. All that talk about investing in things and helping out with the kids was just that, talk. He was flat broke."

Hudson's eyebrows went up, and he whistled. "That would've come as one hell of a shock to Kendra."

The sheriff nodded. "If you folks will excuse me, I think it's time we had a chat with Mrs. Edwards. I thank you for your time Ms...Sunny. I'll be in touch if I need anything else." He nodded to Rhys and Hudson. They nodded back, and Striker left.

"Well," Rhys said, "I don't know about you, but I'm starving. What do you say I head on over to the diner and get us some real breakfast?"

Sunny's belly growled loudly, which made her laugh.

Hudson smiled. "I'd say that was a yes."

Rhys grinned. "I like a woman with an appetite. Besides, I promised Clara I'd swing by and bring her over. I'll see you in a bit." He gave them a wave and walked out.

"Looks like it's just you and me," Hudson said. "It's about damn time because I've been waiting all morning to do this." He leaned down, slid a hand behind her head, and captured her lips in a fierce kiss.

Sunny's heart started beating double-time in her chest. She wanted Hudson so badly it was painful, but she needed to face reality. She broke off the kiss. "Hudson, we should talk."

Hudson's eyes narrowed, but he kept silent as he sat down on the side of Sunny's bed.

"I want to thank you for saving my life." Hudson opened his mouth, but she put her hand up. "Let me finish. You *did* save my life, and I owe you. And I also owe you for your mother's truck." She frowned. "But Hudson, you lied to me. I get why you did it and, you're right, I would've refused if you offered your help. But you lied. I need someone who will always be honest no matter what.

"And you're going to leave town in a few weeks when your mom gets back, and I'm...not. I'm going to stay here because I owe it to Gran and because I want to be close to her. As much as I would love to be back working at a better job and furthering my career, it's not in the cards right now."

She swallowed the tears that were climbing her throat. Her heart was breaking in her chest, but she had to get the words out. "I know your job is overseas and you're happy there and I'm thrilled you found something you love. I don't want a part-time relationship with someone who's halfway around the world. So, thank you, but—"

"Stop." Hudson put his hand over her mouth. "You aren't dumping me. I won't let you. I was a fool to leave you before, but I'm not enough of a fool to make the same mistake twice. I'll apologize until the day I die for underestimating your ability to take care of yourself and for lying to you. You're right. I should've told you the truth from the very beginning. I promise I'll never lie to you ever again. You have proved beyond a shadow of a doubt you don't need rescuing."

"Hudson, I can't leave—"

He shook his head. "I know. I'm not asking you to. After almost losing you last night, I called my boss back in the Middle East and quit."

Sunny blinked. Panic gripped her heart in its icy fingers. He had quit his job for her. He would resent her in no time. Hudson did not want to be a rancher. She put her hand on his chest and shook her head. "No. No. No. Hudson you hate ranching. You can't stay here. You'll hate me for it."

He covered her hand with his, cradling it. "Will you let me finish?"

She bit her lip and nodded.

Hudson smiled. "I quit because I realized something else last night. I like being home. It makes me happy. I love being able to ride again. And I love not being shot at, well, at least not on a regular basis."

Sunny laugh and then hiccupped.

"Most of all I love you. You're what's been missing from my life. I need you Sunny. You make me very happy."

Tears ran down her face. "Hudson, I ... What will you do? You hate ranching."

"I already thought of that. Hank Patterson offered me a full-time position with his company, and if I can drum up enough business over here, then I might even open my own branch. He's been thinking of expanding over this way. So I'll still be doing what I love, and I'll get to be with you if you'll have me."

Sunny was speechless. She wanted to believe it was true. She wanted to believe that Hudson loved her, that he was going to stay with her, but it all seemed so unreal. Too perfect.

Hudson frowned and tilted his head. "Ah, Sunny, um if you don't want to be with me..."

Sunny reached up and fisted his sweater, pulling him to her. "Hudson Riggs, I want to be with you always," she whispered and then kissed him long and hard.

EPILOGUE

SUNNY DISCONNECTED her cell and grinned. Life was good.

"What's the smile about?" Hudson asked as he walked through the door with a mug of tea in his hand. He set it down on the desk and swooped in for a quick kiss.

"I spoke with Jameson Drake, my old boss, again. Remember how I told him about the spa and it could be a real moneymaker with proper management?"

Hudson leaned his butt against the desk on Sunny's left side. "I remember. What did he say?"

"It turns out the FBI was investigating the manager of the spa for embezzlement. He ran off with several million dollars. No one has seen him in weeks. The assistant manager was trying to keep it going, but it's a real mess."

"Wow. Did the guy leave the country?"

"That's the thinking, I guess, but that's not the best part. Drake approached the owner and offered to buy the spa from him at a cut-rate price, and the guy agreed. He's finished with the business. So now Drake owns the spa Sunny was grinning like a Cheshire cat.

Hudson's eyebrow went up. "And?"

"And he wants me to redo it, bring it up to his standards, and then run it. You're looking at the new manager of The Wellness Retreat at Canyon Springs!"

Hudson let out a whoop as he scooped Sunny right out of her chair and gave her a huge hug. "Honey, that's awesome! I'm so happy for you!!"

Sunny hugged him back. "I know. I'm so happy. It's going to be so much work and yet so much fun."

Hudson set her down on her feet and grinned at her. "So, if you're going to be super busy, then I should probably take advantage now of any free time you have."

Sunny laughed and then tried to look serious. "That might be a good idea. What exactly did you have in mind?"

Hudson leaned down and whispered in her ear. Heat bloomed across her cheeks as he told her in vivid detail what he had planned.

"Ah, I think I can make time for that," she said as he straightened up.

"You better!" he growled and then swooped and captured her lips in a scorching kiss.

THE END

ALSO BY LORI MATTHEWS

Callahan Security Series

Break and Enter

Smash and Grab

Hit and Run

BROTHERHOOD PROTECTORS

ORIGINAL SERIES BY ELLE JAMES

Brotherhood Protectors Series

ABOUT ELLE JAMES

ELLE JAMES also writing as MYLA JACKSON is a *New York Times* and *USA Today* Bestselling author of books including cowboys, intrigues and paranormal adventures that keep her readers on the edges of their seats. With over eighty works in a variety of sub-genres and lengths she has published with Harlequin, Samhain, Ellora's Cave, Kensington, Cleis Press, and Avon. When she's not at her computer, she's traveling, snow skiing, boating, or riding her ATV, dreaming up new stories. Learn more about Elle James at www.ellejames.com

Website | Facebook | Twitter | GoodReads | Newsletter | BookBub | Amazon

Follow Elle!
www.ellejames.com
ellejames@ellejames.com

facebook.com/ellejamesauthor
twitter.com/ElleJamesAuthor

Printed in Great Britain
by Amazon